PRAISE F

Forever Mine

Warn your people not to disturb you then settle in and start reading this phenomenal, heartfelt, swoony romance today! Your romantic heart will thank you.

— BOOKADDICT

The Prince I Love to Hate

The Prince I Love To Hate is an absolute must read! This romcom will have you rooting for Niamh and Olivier right from their hilarious first meeting.

— HARLEQUIN BOOK JUNKIE BLOG

Oopsie Daisy

Quirky, fun, witty, hilarious! Iris Morland always manages to get me to laugh out loud.

— WHISPERING CHAPTERS

He Loves Me, He Loves Me Not

A hilarious, sexy and heartwarming romantic comedy...you do not want to miss this fun, feel-good romance.

— MARY DUBÉ, CONTEMPORARILY EVER AFTER

...refreshing, funny, emotionally charged, and very entertaining to read.

— CAROL, TIL THE LAST PAGE

There is humor, there is heart and there is heat in this story! I absolutely loved it! . . . Mari and Liam delivered. Yowza, their chemistry was palpable.

— BIBLIOPHILE CHLOE

Petal Plucker

Funny, charming, and utterly captivating! I devoured this sparkling read.

— ANNIKA MARTIN, NEW YORK TIMES BESTSELLING AUTHOR

Petal Plucker was funny, entertaining, fresh and fan-yourself-worthy . . . Their enemies-to-lovers romance is both charming, tender and steamy, and you'll love both of these characters (and their families!) and their sigh-worthy happily ever after.

— MARY DUBÉ, CONTEMPORARILY EVER AFTER

Morland has created a masterpiece of a romance . . . one of my favorite [books] of the year.

— CRISTIINA READS

Humorous, raunchy, and refreshing, Petal Plucker has rightfully earned its way, in my opinion, as one of the best romantic comedy [books] this year.

— CAROL, TIL THE LAST PAGE

My One and Only

This book was gripping, well written & the chemistry between the characters sizzled throughout this wonderful read.

— AMAZON REVIEW

ALSO BY IRIS MORLAND

STANDALONES

Always a Bridesmaid, Never a Plus-One

LOVE EVERLASTING

including

HAZEL ISLAND

One Perfect Summer

Forever Mine

My Heart to Keep

Love Is Here to Stay

THE YOUNGERS

Then Came You

Taking a Chance on Love

All I Want Is You

My One and Only

THE THORNTONS

The Nearness of You

The Very Thought of You

If I Can't Have You

Dream a Little Dream of Me

Someone to Watch Over Me

Till There Was You

I'll Be Home for Christmas

THE HEIR AFFAIR DUET

The Prince I Love to Hate

The Princess I Hate to Love

HERON'S LANDING

Say You're Mine

All I Ask of You

Make Me Yours

Hold Me Close

THE FLOWER SHOP SISTERS

War of the Roses

Petal Plucker

He Loves Me, He Loves Me Not

Oopsie Daisy

To Amy,

ALWAYS A BRIDESMAID, NEVER A PLUS-ONE

IRIS MORLAND

Happy Reading!
♡ Iris

BLUE VIOLET PRESS LLC

This book is a work of fiction. The names, characters, places and incidents are products of the writer's imagination or have been used fictitiously and are not to be constructed as real. Any resemblance to persons, living or dead, actual events, locales or organizations is entirely coincidental.

Always a Bridesmaid, Never a Plus-One

Published by Blue Violet Press LLC
Seattle, Washington

Cover design by Qamber Designs

For everyone who loves to talk about weddings as much as I do. This book is for you.

ALWAYS A BRIDESMAID, NEVER A PLUS-ONE

CHAPTER ONE

ANNA

As a wedding planner and bridesmaid-for-hire, I'd seen a lot of crazy things at people's weddings over the years.

Drunk groom who could barely remember his own name? Check.

Florist who used the one flower the bride was deathly allergic to? Check.

A ringbearer swallowing the ring right before the ceremony? Check.

Nothing fazed me. I'd seen it all. Family drama? I could diffuse the tensest arguments ever. Hysterical crying because the bride's dress no longer fit? Nothing a little wizardry and fabric tape couldn't handle.

Tonight was my one-hundredth wedding. Pleased with myself, I made the fatal mistake of paying more attention to the plate of fajitas in front of me than to whomever was standing to say a toast to the bride and groom.

I clapped after the best man made his toast. He even managed to get a few laughs out of the crowd. After he and the groom slapped each other's backs instead of a full hug, I didn't notice another person standing up.

To be fair, Granny Ruth was so small I'd been surprised she hadn't needed a booster seat. Despite her small stature, she was also one of the most terrifying people I'd ever met.

The first time I met her, she told me that I was too skinny and too young to be a wedding planner. What being too skinny had to do with planning someone's wedding, I didn't know.

"To my grandson," Granny Ruth said in a voice that made the crowd instantly go quiet. She raised her glass, her gaze solely on her grandson. "I'm so happy for you," she said. She wiped away a tear.

I wasn't moved. I froze in anticipation.

I glanced at the bride, Meredith, whose face had gone deathly pale. Her groom, Trevor, looked similarly horrified.

"Trevor Eric. My only grandson. I waited for this day my entire life. You look so handsome in your suit. When you broke up with Sarah, we were so heartbroken.

"Such a pretty, smart girl. We thought you'd never get married after that. You told us you loved her so much."

Trevor was grimacing. Meredith shot me a look that said, *Stop her!*

The thing was, I hadn't been paying attention, and I'd let Granny Ruth start talking when I should've kept her from the mic entirely. To be fair, I'd told the DJ who not to give the microphone to, but apparently that list had been forgotten.

Granny Ruth gestured to someone in the back. From the corner of my eye, I could see a woman with dark hair and her arms crossed. She also happened to be wearing white.

Who invited the ex-girlfriend? I thought wildly.

"Then one day you brought home your new girlfriend," continued Granny Ruth, eliciting a few chuckles from the crowd. "She's not a Catholic, though. Not like Sarah. I'd always dreamed that one day you'd marry in the church."

The mother of the groom tried to shush her, but to no avail. Granny Ruth merely shook off the offending hand.

"But we're glad now you didn't marry in the church. Your girlfriend wouldn't have been able to wear white like she did today."

Silence. I heard a buzzing in my ears. Then I sprang from my seat and snagged the mic from Granny Ruth.

"Thank you for that speech," I said as cheerfully as possible. "Let's give another round of applause for the happy couple!"

The crowd gave a few halfhearted claps, but I kept clapping until everyone else followed suit. I could feel Granny Ruth glaring at my back. If looks could kill, I was sure I would've been dead on the floor already from her steely gaze.

I hurried to Meredith, whispering in her ear, "I'm so sorry—"

Meredith shook off my touch. "It's fine." She pushed her chair back in a huff.

When Trevor didn't immediately follow her, she snapped at her new husband, "Are you coming?"

He mumbled something under his breath, casting me a resigned look.

I could tell that the tension was worsening as Meredith

and Trevor began to cut the cake. Meredith wasn't looking at her husband at all, while Trevor looked vaguely constipated.

The cake was four tiers, a white tower of frosting, flowers, and an adorable cake topper that included the couple's dopey chocolate lab, Mickey.

I rubbed the back of my neck. "Not your best work, Dyer," I muttered to myself.

I needed to salvage this. I hurried to the DJ and told him to start playing Journey, the couple's favorite band.

"We need to get this party started," I told him. "Liven things up after that."

The DJ shrugged as the sounds of "Don't Stop Believin'" filled the banquet hall.

The cake cutting fortunately didn't turn into Meredith stabbing anyone with the cake knife. When Trevor tried to feed her a piece, though, she turned her face away and immediately returned to her seat at the bridal table.

I racked my brain, knowing that the mood of the wedding was slipping through my fingers.

I could've cheerfully wrung Granny Ruth's neck. She looked especially smug right now. Surely it wasn't illegal to strangle an old lady when you had a good reason?

My palms were starting to sweat, my heart pounding with anxiety, when the universe decided to be nice to me for a moment.

A waiter was cutting the cake for the rest of the guests when another waiter, carrying multiple trays of dirty dishes, tripped over the cake-cutting waiter's feet. The trays—and the dish-carrying waiter—came crashing down in a loud heap.

One of the trays went flying like a deadly frisbee. I watched in horror as it headed straight for the cake.

I reacted solely on instinct. I ran, my legs pumping, and threw myself in front of the tray. It hit me straight in the stomach.

But when I fell to the floor and saw that the cake was still standing, I didn't care that I'd made a fool out of myself.

I'd saved the cake from utter destruction. That was what mattered. My dignity was a worthy sacrifice.

Various guests were standing over me. When Meredith came over, she gazed down at me, her mouth wide open.

Then she started giggling.

"Oh, Anna," she kept saying, the laughter spilling out of her. "That was amazing. And insane."

One of the guests helped me up. I realized too late that I'd gotten splashed with some unknown liquid.

Cola? I wrinkled my nose. No, it was wine. Great. I'd never get that stain out of my dress. Good thing it was a dress I didn't care about wearing a second time.

I was muttering to myself when someone handed me a napkin. I dabbed at the wet stain, all the while knowing there was hardly any point. I'd experienced enough stains of all sorts at weddings to know this one wasn't going to come out without some major effort.

I went to the bathroom, relieved that it was empty. I cleaned myself up as best I could, but when I saw that even my shoes were now stained, I gave up. I wasn't going to win this battle.

I fixed my hair in the mirror and reapplied my lipstick. Just because my entire outfit was now splashed with wine didn't mean my face shouldn't still be presentable. I also didn't want people to think I was flustered.

When I exited the bathroom, I hesitated. The raucous music from the reception was so loud that I could feel the bass vibrating the floor. I heard cheers, and then I was heading in the opposite direction.

It was a cool night. People think that SoCal is always warm, but they don't realize how cold it can get at night in the desert. In my damp dress, it didn't take long for me to start shivering.

"That was a nice save back there," said a male voice.

I jumped. And because my bad luck was infinite tonight, I found myself nearly toppling backward into the grass like a newborn giraffe.

"Whoa!" The man grabbed my forearm, hauling me up. "You okay?"

It took me a moment to sort through what was going on. The first thing I noticed was that this man smelled amazing. Sandalwood, with something else that was spicy. I inhaled deeply.

Then I realized that he was still holding my arm, and I was plastered against him.

I disentangled myself, feeling like an idiot. "I swear I'm not usually this clumsy," I blurted. I felt sweat break out on my forehead. "This is just an off night."

"You weren't the clumsy one in there." The man gestured toward the event hall. "You dove in front of that cake like some kind of superhero. Although I'm not sure it was really worth it. It was just a cake, after all."

I gaped at him. "It's their *wedding cake*. You only get one wedding cake. And Meredith especially wanted to take home the top tier to freeze and eat on their one-year anniversary."

The man made a face. Despite the multitude of streetlamps, cars and buildings that kept the city lit up like a Christmas tree, I couldn't see this man's features well.

I could tell that he was tall, and he was wearing a nice suit. His hair was dark. That was about all the details I could glean.

When he stepped into the light, though, I felt like somebody had thrown another glass of wine. This time, into my face.

This man—he was *fucking gorgeous.*

"Who wants to eat a half-frozen cake from a year ago?" he was saying. "Does anybody still do that?"

I shook myself internally. "Yeah, lots of couples do." I looked him up and down. "Are you married?"

His grin was easy, and it was annoying how handsome it made him. "Nah. That's not my vibe."

"Love isn't your vibe?"

"Who says marriage is a requirement for love?"

I waved a hand. "Any man who says he isn't into marriage is really saying that he doesn't like commitments in general. It's doublespeak."

"Really? You speak for all men?"

"Do you know how many weddings I've been involved with? How many grooms I've seen who've acted like their lives were over on the day of their wedding? Too many, I'll tell you that."

He made a face. "Then why get married?"

"Peer pressure. Your family's expectations. Money. Kids. Tax benefits. All kinds of reasons."

"If you're trying to convince me to agree with the concept of marriage," the handsome stranger said wryly, "you're doing a shit job of it."

I laughed. "If it makes you feel better, most grooms are excited and in love with their brides. And I've learned when to say no to a couple if I get a feeling that one of them isn't as gung-ho as the other."

"Very wise of you."

I felt his gaze on me, and it made my skin prickle. When his gaze dropped to my cleavage, my pussy clenched. Yes, *clenched.*

I didn't even know this guy's name, and I wanted him to stick his hand down my panties right here and now.

Based on his expression, he seemed to be reading my mind. He moved closer, until I was pressed against the warm, brick wall.

"So," he drawled, "are you married?"

I held up my ringless hand. "Nope."

"A wedding planner who isn't married. Isn't that an oxymoron?"

"Planning a wedding isn't the same thing as getting married."

His lips quirked. "True."

I felt his breath on my forehead, and I couldn't stop myself from tilting my head back. Did I want him to kiss me? *Yeah, I do.*

My logical brain wanted to remind me that I couldn't just bounce from this wedding to hook up with one of the guests. Meredith was probably wondering where the hell I was.

Shut up, brain. Just give me this for once.

I hadn't had sex in way too long. I was fairly certain I had cobwebs growing from my pussy at this point. Having a man this close? It was heady. It was overwhelming.

"What's your name?" the man asked, then he kissed me gently behind my ear.

It took me way too long to croak, "Anna."

I could feel him smile. "Nice to meet you." He licked at my pulse. "I'm Rowan."

He kissed my neck, my body on fire. My brain, however, was filling with the sound of alarm bells, like a fire truck's siren coming closer and closer.

"Rowan?" My voice was hoarse. That name sounded familiar… "What's your last name?"

Rowan stepped back, giving me an odd look. "Caldwell. Why?"

"Oh my God." I covered my eyes, wishing I could melt into the wall behind me. "You're my best friend's ex-boyfriend."

CHAPTER TWO

ANNA

At brunch the following Sunday, Melanie Wilson, my best friend of over a decade, choked on her avocado toast.

It was my fault, really. She'd taken a bite at the exact moment I'd revealed that I'd run into Rowan. Her ex-boyfriend.

Melanie coughed so loudly that, over the din of the brunch service, other restaurant goers turned their gazes toward us. I pushed her mimosa toward her, and she downed its contents in seconds.

"Rowan?" she gasped. "You're kidding. Tell me you're kidding."

I considered telling her I had been joking, Rowan had probably moved to some far-off island years ago, of course it hadn't been him—

"It was him." I grimaced. "He confirmed it three times."

"Oh my God." Melanie was now downing not only her glass of water, but mine, too. When she noticed that an older woman was staring at her, she snapped, "Take a picture, it'll last longer!"

The woman huffed and returned to her eggs Benedict with a sour frown. I shot her an apologetic look.

"I haven't heard that comeback since the nineties," I said, trying to lighten the mood.

Melanie just rolled her eyes.

Melanie had never been the calmest person. Although she was unfailingly loyal and pretty much down to try anything, she had a quick, fiery temper. I'd always been the one to defuse situations where Melanie had wanted to go on the attack. It was probably why I'd gotten so good at planning weddings.

Her temper was also why I'd confessed about the Rowan incident now. I was a terrible liar, and it was better to let Melanie know. Besides, Rowan and I hadn't done anything. Once I'd realized who he was, I'd practically sprinted back inside to the wedding, leaving him totally confused.

I'm sure you're wondering: how had I not recognized my best friend's ex? When Melanie and Rowan had been dating—about five years ago now—I'd been in San Diego for that year to help my parents. My dad had gotten in a bad car accident, and my mom couldn't care for him by herself.

By the time I'd returned to Pasadena, I'd met Rowan one time before the pair had broken up.

Besides, the man I'd remembered hadn't been as dynamic as the Rowan I'd met at the wedding. The Rowan Melanie had introduced me to five years ago had been standoffish. He'd barely said five words to me the entire time we'd eaten dinner together.

When he'd ended things, I hadn't been surprised. I hadn't told Melanie that, of course. She'd been devastated for months.

"I thought he'd moved away," said Melanie. "I could've sworn I'd seen an update on Facebook about him."

I shrugged. "Apparently not. And apparently we know some of the same people."

Melanie took a large bite of her toast. "So, how did he look? Was he ugly and fat now? Please tell me he is."

I looked heavenward. *He's even hotter than I remember him?* Yeah, Melanie would love to hear that from me.

"He looked about the same," I hedged.

"What about his hairline? I remember he was starting to go bald when we were dating."

"Well, if he is bald now, he has a great toupee."

That remark made Melanie laugh. "Too bad you couldn't yank it off him. Man, I'd love to see him again." Melanie smiled evilly. "Make him squirm. Or cry. Rip off his toupee and then kick him in the balls."

"Let's not get arrested now."

"No jury would convict me."

I just sipped my mimosa.

Melanie stabbed a piece of arugula, making me glad I wasn't a vegetable on her plate right now. She had murder in her eyes.

"Well, if you see him again, promise me you'll tell him to go fuck himself," she said. Based on her tone, it wasn't a request. It was an order.

I cocked an eyebrow. "Mel, I'm not running him over. I can see in your face you'd want me to."

"Just a little bump. Or just a roll over his foot."

I laughed, shaking my head. "You're crazy."

That made her face turn red. She pointed her fork at me. "Don't gaslight me. You know he was a dick to me."

I sobered quickly. How could I forget? I'd spent many nights listening to Melanie cry on the phone, to the point that I'd gone over to her place more than once to check she was okay. She'd lost weight to the point that I'd encouraged her to talk to someone. Melanie, being stubborn, had refused.

I hadn't realized she'd still harbored this much anger, though. It made my gut twist with guilt for flirting—and fantasizing—about Rowan that night. Even though I hadn't even known who he was at the time, I knew Melanie well enough to know she wouldn't be so forgiving of that transgression.

"I know things ended badly between you two. I was there, remember?" I said.

Melanie's expression softened. "I know you were. You picked me up and put me back together." She took my hand and squeezed it. "I'll never forget that. I'm not sure what I would've done without you."

"Probably burned his house down."

She smiled evilly. "Probably." Her expression turned serious. "I mean it, though: stay away from him. He seemed so amazing at first, but when he started showing his true colors, everything changed. He froze me out. It was like, one day he just…stopped caring. I tried so hard to get him to care about me again, but he only turned colder and colder."

"You guys weren't compatible."

"Maybe. But he also wasn't interested in saving the relationship. He made the decision without even consulting me, and then it took him months to man up and end it." Melanie's mouth twisted. "Even when I'd begged him to tell me what was wrong."

I sighed. "I doubt I'll see him again."

"But if you do. . ."

"I'll scowl at him every chance I get. I do so solemnly swear." I crossed my heart for emphasis.

Melanie's mood lightened soon after, especially once I began telling her about the shenanigans at the wedding. Melanie had been my biggest cheerleader when I'd decided to be a wedding planner and bridesmaid-for-hire.

She'd even given me money as a birthday gift to fund the business. When I made it big, she'd wanted me to use my connections to meet Ryan Reynolds.

"Pretty sure he's married," I'd told her, laughing.

"So? I don't want to sleep with him. I just want him to tell me something sarcastic and maybe sign my boobs for good measure."

So when Melanie asked me for something—like avoiding her ex-boyfriend Rowan Caldwell—I had good reason to say yes.

I SPENT the rest of the day and evening working. Although I worked for myself, it also meant that my hours weren't the typical eight-to-five, Monday-through-Friday schedule. That was especially true during wedding season, usually from April through October.

As it was now early March, I was in the thick of

confirming details for my first weddings of the busy season. It also meant that I planned bachelorette parties for the bride, went dress shopping with her, and also provided a buffer between her and her family if necessary.

When I'd first researched starting my business, I hadn't even known that bridesmaids-for-hire were a thing. But the more I researched, the more it made sense to me. Bridesmaids, and especially maids of honor, shouldered a ton of responsibility.

Where once upon a time being a bridesmaid just meant wearing an ugly dress and walking down the aisle, now it meant coordinating multiday bachelorette trips. Some coordinated a wedding shower—or three!—for the bride. You paid for your dress, your shoes, your hair, your makeup.

You supported the bride through all the complicated emotions that came up regarding weddings. And then brides who expected their friends to lose weight so that the whole bridal party had a—in their words—a *cohesive* look?

It was no wonder some brides preferred to hire a bridesmaid to fulfill that role than to subject their friends or family to it. Thus, that was how I'd realized I could fill a niche where I was the one telling everybody else what to do. Besides the bride, that is.

After sending the last email of the night, I took a glass of wine with me to bed as I started reading a new romance novel I'd just bought. The wine was soon forgotten, however, as I found myself sucked into the story.

Well, maybe not the story so much as the sex scenes. This author knew how to write some five-star smut. I was practically fanning myself before I'd even reached page twenty-five.

"Lord, I need to get laid," I muttered to myself as I pushed the blankets off. I then glanced at my window, which was open, and considered. It was a warm night, but leaving it open meant I'd have to be very, very quiet.

I finally got up, shut the window, and pulled down the blinds. I might be horny, but I wasn't *indecent.* Besides, the last thing I needed was some rando on the street to hear my giant-ass vibrator humming at full speed.

I pulled out my Hitachi wand, an absurdly large vibrator that you literally had to plug into the wall, and kept reading. My pussy tingled as I read, the scene where the hero had the heroine over his lap, spanking her at the same time he pushed a butt plug into her ass.

I pressed the vibrator against my clit, my toes curling as I closed my eyes. I imagined myself as the heroine, writhing on that lap, feeling the pressure of the butt plug at the same time his rough fingers rubbed my clit—

My eyes flew open when I realized the man I was picturing was none other than Rowan Caldwell. I could see that arrogant smirk on his handsome face; I could even imagine his cheeks slightly flushed as he rubbed me harder and harder.

I could feel my orgasm building deep inside my pelvis. When I imagined Rowan spanking me the moment before I was about to come, I bit the inside of my cheek to keep from screaming.

I never said you could come yet, I could hear him saying. *Bad girls come without asking.*

I begged under my breath, fantasy and reality colliding together dangerously. I felt the quick sting of his hand against my ass at the same time I lifted the vibrator away from my clit before I came for real.

I felt him spread my ass cheeks, pressing on the plug as he simultaneously began fondling my pussy again. When he began to rub my clit—the vibrator now pressed firmly against me—I started to shudder within moments.

Ask me, he said in my mind. *Beg for it.*

"Please," I whispered. "Please, Rowan."

He smiled. And then I came so hard that I had to bury my face into my pillow to muffle my scream.

It took me a while to come back to earth. By the time I'd put away my vibrator, reopened my window to let in the cool air, I felt the weight of reality crash down on me.

"Oh, God," I said, covering my face. "Did I seriously just do that?"

I felt my cheeks heat in embarrassment. Now, I'd certainly fantasized about plenty of men while getting off, but the fact that Rowan Caldwell was still so forefront in my mind? That wasn't good. In fact, it was very, very bad.

You're not going to see him again anyway, I reassured myself after I'd turned off my bedside lamp. *So it doesn't matter. And it's not like you'd ever tell Melanie about this, right?*

I shuddered, but this time, not with pleasure. No, Melanie would never know. I'd go to the grave before I'd admit to her that I'd come thinking about her terrible ex-boyfriend.

CHAPTER THREE

ROWAN

As I gazed upon the land I'd bought five years ago, I never once had the thought to myself: *Let's make this a wedding venue.*

"It's perfect," my best friend, Alejandro Perez, said. He gestured to the expanse in front of us. "How can you not see it?"

I frowned. I'd bought this piece of land located north of Santa Clarita, some forty miles from downtown Los Angeles. It was wide-open country—literally the middle of fucking nowhere—and it showed. Where I wasn't growing orange trees, it was open, dry fields. I could see a few cows roaming in the distance.

"I really doubt Em is going to be excited to get married in a random-ass field," I said dryly.

A cow mooed, as if agreeing with me.

Alejo, being Alejo, wasn't listening to me. I'd known him since we'd been kids, and he'd always been the type of person with big ideas. Sometimes the ideas turned into gold; other times, they turned into disasters. But to be fair to

Alejo, he often had good ideas that other people dismissed, only for Alejo to prove them wrong.

It helped that Alejo was a good-looking guy, generally speaking. Or so many women had told me whenever we'd gone out drinking. Alejo had charm. He could convince nearly anyone—men, women, children—that the sky was green if he had a mind to it.

Right now, though, I really, really didn't need my best friend to convince me that I'd made a mistake. Alejo fucking *loved* to gloat, the asshole.

"It needs work, obviously." Alejo was striding across my property like he owned the place. "We'd have to rent all the furniture we'd need, but it'll still save us money in the long run."

I doubted that, but it wasn't my wedding.

The thought of weddings made me think about that gorgeous wedding planner I'd nearly felt up at a cousin's marriage two weeks ago.

She's your ex's best friend. Don't even think about it.

"Did you hear me?" Alejo was practically sprinting from inside the barn now. When had he even gone in there? The man was like the Energizer Bunny. He never fucking stopped.

I wiped the beads of sweat from my forehead. I needed to get on with my work, not dawdle around imagining where to put wedding arches. The hell was a wedding arch anyway?

"Nope," I replied, making Alejo shake his head. "You talk too much anyway."

"I was saying, are you on board? You wouldn't have to do anything. Our coordinator would."

"On my land? Doubtful. I'm not going to let some wedding planner come out here and start fucking around with my land. I'll have to supervise."

"Then we'll pay you."

I was annoyed that I was tempted by the offer. Last year's crop hadn't been great, and my savings was dwindling. An influx of cash would be helpful. But then I'd have to admit as much to Alejo.

"I'll think about it," I hedged.

"I'll even write the contract."

That made me snort. "And fuck me over in the process? Hardly. I'll ask a lawyer friend of mine to draft something for us."

"So that's a yes?" Alejo's dumb face looked way too excited now.

"It's a *maybe.* Calm down. I still think it's a terrible idea."

"No, you don't. You're just mad you didn't think of it yourself."

I couldn't disagree. Although I had no real interest in making my farm into a wedding venue, it would certainly bring in a lot more money. When Alejo had told me that weddings were a billion-dollar industry, my eyeballs had nearly popped straight out of my head.

The hell were these couples spending all that money on? My brain couldn't imagine it.

Alejo gave my shoulder a friendly pat. "Think about it, old man. You know I'm right."

"You're one year younger than me. Stop calling me old man," I groused.

"I call you that because you act like one, not because

you are one." Alejo raised a dark eyebrow. "How's the business going, by the way?"

"I'm not making software-engineer money, if that's what you're asking."

"I still don't totally get why you left AppVille. You were making more than me, or anyone else on our team."

Gazing out onto the horizon, I took in the land I'd bought, the land that I'd gotten so attached to in the past five years. That feeling? No job at some tech company could replace it.

"Because I didn't like the work," I said simply.

"Yeah, but the money—"

"I don't care about money." *What a fucking lie*, my mind pointed out rather unhelpfully.

"Brian was asking about you. Sean just took a job at Google so Brian is sweating his balls off trying to replace him."

"Really? Now, that actually is surprising."

"They offered Sean a whole fuckton of bonuses. Brian tried so damn hard to get him to stay, but no go." Alejo shrugged. "After you left, I think a lot of the other guys felt some major FOMO. Like, why would the senior-ranking software engineer, the guy who'd literally helped start AppVille, leave to grow fucking orange trees?"

"Because I wanted to."

"Well, if you change your mind, Brian will take you back in a heartbeat. He'd probably cry tears of joy." Alejo's lips quirked. "It'd be hilarious."

We'd wandered to my grove of oranges, and I took in the rows and rows of them with a feeling of satisfaction.

Although sometimes in the dark of night I'd wonder if I'd made the right choice, at the moment, I knew that I had.

There weren't many orange groves in existence in Southern California anymore. Seventy years ago, the region had been famous for its citrus trees. It was why Orange County was named as such. But as the region had exploded in population, the groves had gradually disappeared, the acres of trees giving way to housing developments.

My farm was keeping the old ways alive. I'd started growing navel and Valencia oranges initially. I'd considered expanding to lemons and grapefruits in a few years. Regardless of the type of fruit I grew, there was something about seeing the white blossoms on the trees slowly morph into fruit that never failed to amaze me, year after year.

"Tell Brian he needs to stop asking about employees who left years ago," I said finally.

"That's what I say, but he knows we're friends. He probably thinks I could talk you into coming back."

"Brian is a manager with a power complex. He's just pissed I told him off and he couldn't do anything about it."

Alejo laughed. "Probably. Why he'd want you back, I don't know."

Alejo handed me his wedding coordinator's business card. "In case you decide to do this thing. If you do, Em will love you forever."

"She's your fiancée. I don't think you want her to love *me* forever," I replied.

Alejo shrugged. "Happy wife, happy life. Maybe someday you'll understand."

I tucked the card into my pocket without looking at it as

Alejo drove away. I had no idea if I should say yes to this scheme of his. When he'd first asked me about using the farm as his wedding venue, I'd told him there was no way in hell.

But my best friend being the man he was, he'd somehow finagled things so that I was now seriously considering doing it.

I took out the business card Alejo had given me. When I read the name, I swore.

Anna Dyer

To Have and to Hold Weddings

Wedding Coordinator

Surely it was a coincidence? But a quick search online showed me it was, in fact, the exact same woman I'd met at Trevor's wedding.

The woman who also happened to be best friends with my ex-girlfriend.

Sure, Melanie and I hadn't been together in five years. We'd dated for less than a year. But the breakup had been the messiest of all my breakups. Melanie hadn't been inclined to react calmly or kindly when I'd told her I'd wanted to end things.

"You fucking broke up with me over *text message*!" she'd screamed.

Standing in the middle of her apartment, I'd watched her rage and scream at me; her reaction had only given me more good reasons to end things.

Her little Yorkie, Cupcake, barked and growled at my ankles, as if backing up his mistress's tantrum.

"Look, I know things haven't been great lately," Melanie was saying, tears streaming down her face, "but to text me!

Did you even fucking read what you wrote before you hit send?"

I didn't respond. It was easier, really, not to respond when Melanie was like this.

"Answer me!" Her voice was a screech now. Everyone from here to Santa Monica could probably hear her.

"What's there to say?" I shrugged, even as my heart was pounding inside my chest.

"Seriously? You won't even try to defend yourself? To explain yourself?" Melanie showed me the text I'd sent her.

It read, *This isn't working for me anymore. I want to break up. Sorry.*

I cringed inwardly, rereading the message. "I thought it'd be better. A clean break. No fuss," I said.

"Christ, this isn't a business deal. It's a relationship." Melanie's expression was incredulous. "Are you a fucking robot? Because I'm pretty sure you're heartless."

That stung. She had no idea how much I'd struggled with ending this damn thing: the guilt, the uncertainty, the tangled feelings of resentment and, yes, even love. I'd continued with the relationship way longer than I should have.

"You don't fucking know me," I growled. "I'm leaving."

"Of course you are. That's all you know how to do. Leave!"

I heard something crash against the wall as I left. I was just glad that she hadn't thrown whatever it was at my head.

Staring down at the business card, the memories of Melanie flooded me. Sure, the relationship had been hot and heavy in the beginning. When Melanie wasn't angry, she was fun and spontaneous, things I'd never been good at.

I wandered down the rows of my orange trees, inhaling their sweet scent. So what if I had to work with Melanie's best friend? This would be an entirely professional relationship.

Even as I had that thought, I couldn't help but remember the way Anna had licked her lips as she'd gazed up at me. She'd practically been begging me to kiss her. It had only been me revealing who I was that had stopped us.

Something niggled at the back of my brain. And then, in a flash, I remembered that I'd met Anna once before. The memory was fuzzy around the edges. All I could remember was Melanie's friend—as she'd been at the time—had rolled her eyes at something Melanie had said. Other than that, I hardly paid her any attention.

"And clearly, you made only a vague impression on her," I muttered to myself as I went back inside the house. To my annoyance, that realization smarted.

It was one thing for me not to remember Anna. It was something else entirely for her not to remember *me.* Yes, hypocrisy: thy name was Rowan Caldwell.

I took out the business card, as if it could impart advice just from touching it.

Alejo and Em wanted their wedding here. I wanted to make that a reality.

If it meant keeping my hands off the pretty wedding planner?

So be it.

CHAPTER FOUR

ANNA

I was running late. I *never* ran late, especially to wedding planning meetings.

I was that person who responded to emails within a few hours, if not minutes. I was that person who was often five to ten minutes early.

But today was just not going well. Sure, I could blame it on traffic—everywhere in LA was notorious for its terrible traffic—but it wasn't even for that reason. I'd simply lost track of time.

Anna Dyer never lost track of time.

I nearly ran over a pedestrian jaywalking as I searched for a parking space near the cafe in downtown Pasadena. Of course, the only spot available on the street was in between two massive SUVs, and even my little sedan couldn't parallel park into that space.

This meant going around the block three times until I finally gave up. I ended up parking inside a garage, where I'd probably have to pay an ungodly amount.

I was sweaty and irritated when I entered the cafe. I forced myself to stop, take a deep breath, and check my hair and makeup before going further. I couldn't let my clients know when I was frazzled. Weddings were anxiety-inducing enough. If your wedding planner was also a mess, your wedding would probably be one, too.

"Over here!" A blond woman, tall and leggy, waved from the back of the cafe. A man with black hair was seated facing away from me. He was most likely Emily's fiancé, Alejandro.

"Emily Lange?" I asked.

"Yep!" Emily bounced from her seat, shaking my hand with such enthusiasm that I couldn't help but compare her to a golden retriever. Except this golden retriever had model-esque cheekbones, a perfect blowout, and a Prada bag that made me drool when I noticed it.

"Anna Dyer." I smiled.

Alejandro stood up, and when I turned toward him, I nearly fell over from surprise.

This wasn't Alejandro. This was—

"The hell are you doing here?" I blurted.

Rowan Caldwell gave me a lazy grin. "Nice to see you again." He put his hand out.

I shook it, trying to hide my discombobulation.

"You've already met?" Emily's wide blue eyes widened further. "What a nice coincidence!"

Rowan sat back down, gesturing for me to sit likewise.

"I need some coffee. Anyone want something?" I asked.

After I was given their coffee orders, I went to stand in line, forcing my racing thoughts to slow down.

Why Rowan Caldwell was with Emily, and not her fiancé, I didn't know. I hoped it was just a random occurrence. Maybe Emily had spotted Rowan at a table and had invited him over. Although I doubted that Rowan would be interested in talking about weddings.

Just the thought of boring him to tears, talking about timelines, color schemes, dresses? That thought made me smile evilly.

"Alejo had a business meeting come up that he couldn't miss," Emily explained after I'd returned with all three coffee orders.

While Emily and I had ordered lattes, Rowan had gotten a boring cup of black coffee. Why did I have the feeling he considered mayonnaise an exotic condiment?

"I'm sorry to hear that," I replied. "I was looking forward to meeting him."

"He wanted me to say that he'll be there next time. He's just as excited about the wedding as I am. Last night, we were looking at bridesmaids' dresses. I swear, he has more opinions about dresses than I do."

Rowan snorted. "Oh, how the mighty have fallen," he said.

"There's nothing wrong with the guy being interested in his own wedding," I pointed out.

Rowan raised an eyebrow. "There's interested, and then there's being way too excited."

Emily just laughed. "So says the perpetual bachelor. When you meet the right woman, you'll probably do the same thing."

Rowan just shrugged and drank his boring coffee.

"You never did say why Rowan is here," I said, shooting Rowan a glance.

"Oh? Didn't I say? He's the owner of our venue. I mean, it's his orange farm. It's never been a wedding venue before, so we'll have a lot of work to spruce it up," said Emily.

My stomach sank into my toes. It was one thing to run into Rowan at weddings and coffee shops, but this meant we'd have to work together. For months. The wedding was over a year away. A cold sweat broke out on my forehead.

Rowan was smirking, as if reading my thoughts. "I look forward to working with you," he said blandly.

"Same," I said in a too-cheery tone.

Emily and I talked about the overall wedding aesthetic, Rowan interjecting here and there. But when only an hour had passed, Emily glanced at her phone and gasped.

"Oh crap. I totally forgot that I have an appointment. I'm getting my lashes done, and my esthetician is booked out six months. It's impossible to get in lately," said Emily as she packed her bag. To me, she said, "Can you send me everything in an email about what we talked about?"

"Of course," I replied.

"And you two, you can talk getting permits and what-not." Emily waved a hand. "See you guys later. Sorry for running out like this!"

And before either of us could say goodbye, Emily was gone. Rowan and I blinked at each other. It had rather been like a tornado had just ripped through and then promptly disappeared.

"Do you want another one?" asked Rowan.

"What?"

He pointed. "A coffee thing." He held up his empty mug. "I need more if we're talking about permits."

I gave him my order, which made him roll his eyes: an oat milk latte with no foam and with an extra shot. "How did coffee get so complicated?" he muttered to himself.

When he returned, I'd already gotten out all of my folders with documents about getting permits and what a venue needed to have to be up to code.

As Rowan looked through the list, he turned a little pale. "Do I need a permit if I'm only doing their wedding?"

"If you're charging them, you probably will. Although I'd have to check with the county. You're in Santa Clarita, right?"

Rowan harrumphed, which I assumed meant *yes*.

"You don't sound all that enthused about the idea," I ventured.

"I'm just skeptical."

"Of what?"

"They think they can transform my place into some magical wedding venue, and I'm not convinced it'll match their vision." He scowled. "And then who gets the blame? Me."

That remark made me laugh. "No, you won't. It'll be *me*. You just have to stand back and watch."

Even as I said the words, I knew Rowan was probably the last person to just "stand back and watch." He'd probably micromanage the entire project. Just the thought of that made my head start to ache.

"It all seems like a huge waste of money." Rowan crossed his arms, which only emphasized his wide chest and shoulders.

I swallowed. I forced myself to stop staring at the way his T-shirt clung to his body. But I couldn't help but wonder what he looked like underneath his clothes.

"I mean, you're spending all this money on one day. One day! It's insane. When Alejo told me their budget, I nearly had a fucking stroke." Rowan scoffed. "It's fucking crazy."

I could barely restrain an eye roll. I'd heard the exact same thing from so many people over the years. If I'd gotten a dollar every time someone had said something like that, I'd never have to work again.

"What you think is fucking crazy is perfectly fine for other people," I pointed out.

"Why not save that money? Buy a house? Go on a vacation? It's one day."

"Just because you don't understand something, that doesn't make it less valuable to other people," I snapped.

Rowan finally seemed to realize I was annoyed. "Look, I'm not criticizing your job—"

"You're also talking about something you literally know nothing about."

"I know when people are getting shafted. They're led to believe that their relationship is doomed unless they spend thousands of dollars on a wedding."

"Look," I said, leaning toward Rowan, "I'm not going to try to convince you weddings are worthwhile. Everybody is different. But if you're really going to host your friends' wedding, you need to get your head out of your ass. Be supportive. Don't be a dick about their choices. That's the number-one rule of weddings: support the couple in whatever *they* want. Period. That's it."

Rowan blinked. Then he let out a surprised laugh. "That was a very convincing speech. Almost like you've had to say it before."

I sniffed. "Too many people—especially men—think weddings are frivolous because they're centered mostly around women."

"Are you seriously telling me I'm being sexist right now?"

I smiled. "If the shoe fits."

He muttered something unintelligible under his breath. I only smiled wider. *Maybe this whole thing is going to be a total blast.*

Rowan seemed deep in thought as I opened my laptop and began typing up the notes from earlier.

"I still don't get the appeal," he said finally, "but I also get your point about keeping your mouth shut. It's not about me. It's about Alejo and Em."

"You're smarter than you look, Mr. Caldwell."

"Thanks for the compliment," was his wry response.

We discussed the details of getting his farm up to scratch for a wedding. Mostly, it was figuring out what we were going to do about mundane—but necessary—details. Where would people park? And how many bathrooms were available for guests' use? Given that Rowan only had a bathroom in his private residence, it meant we'd have to rent port-a-potties and sink stations.

"For a wedding?" Rowan looked skeptical. "I doubt Em would like that."

"Well, if you want guys peeing in your fields after a few drinks. . ."

He sighed. "I get your point."

But we got into it when I suggested one of his fields could be used as a parking lot. Rowan balked at the idea, suggesting instead that people could park elsewhere and take a shuttle.

"When you have so much land? That makes zero sense," I said.

"And I don't want my land destroyed with people driving all over it."

Despite trying to compromise, we eventually had to drop that particular discussion until we were with Alejo and Emily again.

By the time we'd finished, I was starving, tired, and wondering if I'd made a huge mistake in agreeing to take this wedding on. It was one thing to plan everything. It was another to turn a farm into a usable venue, especially when the owner was such a stick-in-the-mud.

Rowan, to my immense annoyance, followed me to my car. I was about to tell him goodbye when I saw a woman in uniform standing by the front of my car. Worst of all, she was writing me a parking ticket.

"Motherfucker," I hissed. I looked at my phone. "I'm only two minutes over my time! What the fuck!"

Everyone in the city hated parking enforcement. They were the actual, literal worst beings on earth. They'd patrol a small area, waiting in anticipation for your parking to expire. There was no mercy, no grace period. The second they smelled blood, they circled like sharks.

"Ma'am!" I called. "Ma'am! I'm only two minutes late. Could you give me a break?"

The officer didn't look up from her tablet. "This your car?" she asked instead.

"Yeah, it's my car. And my parking just expired. I'm going to move my car right now."

The officer just kept inputting information, glancing at my license plate as she did so.

"Ma'am," said Rowan, blocking my license plate from view. "If you'd just give my friend a warning, we'd appreciate it."

His voice was silky, and when the woman looked up, he gave her a grin that'd melt butter in your mouth. I felt that grin in my entire body.

"Her time expired," the officer stated, but she sounded uncertain now.

"That's true. My friend, you see, she's kind of a ditz. But I know a kind, lovely woman such as yourself understands that some people just don't pay attention to details. Not like you do. I'm sure you're one of the best parking attendants in this city," said Rowan.

I had to bite the inside of my cheek to keep from guffawing. Even worse, the officer seemed to be falling under Rowan's spell.

"I was just named Employee of the Month," she said proudly.

Rowan smiled, his gaze floating down the officer's uniformed body. "I bet you're the best at a lot of things," he murmured.

To my astonishment, the officer tore up the ticket, gave me a stern warning, and then whispered something in Rowan's ear that made him chuckle.

"Seriously?" I said.

"It worked, didn't it?" Rowan waved as the officer drove off.

"I don't even know what to say."

He shot me a wry grin. "Better move your car before she changes her mind."

"We wouldn't want that. Then you might have to sleep with her."

CHAPTER FIVE

ROWAN

How had I gotten invited to seemingly every wedding in the city? For the last five years, I'd attended maybe two weddings, tops. Now, suddenly everyone I knew was signing their life away on the dotted line. And for what? A few tax benefits after you paid tens of thousands for a wedding?

This latest wedding was a cousin's. A second cousin, mind you. The only reason I decided to attend was the promise of an open bar, especially since it was all the way up in San Jose, almost six hours north of Santa Clarita. I couldn't remember if I'd even met this cousin before. Why they'd invited me, I had no idea.

And so here I was, watching another ceremony. The musicians were playing a song from some Disney movie as the bridal party made their way down the petal-strewn aisle.

I was trying to place the movie song—*Aladdin*? *Frozen*?—that I almost missed seeing Anna Dyer on the arm of a very skinny groomsman.

"What the hell," I muttered. The woman next to me shot me a glare.

I caught Anna's eye, but she looked away quickly. Now I couldn't restrain a grin.

Maybe this wedding would be fun after all.

I barely watched the bride and groom exchanging vows. I kept watching Anna, who seemed to be the maid of honor. She took the bouquet from the bride; she made sure the bride's train and veil weren't rumpled. She even got the officiant to move out of the way so he wouldn't be in the photo of the first kiss of the newly married couple.

I might think weddings were pointless, but watching Anna, I could tell that they involved more details than I'd realized.

"To celebrate both the joining of Grace and Riley. And to honor those who couldn't be with us today, Grace and Riley would like to release two doves," announced the officiant.

Anna brought forward two cages that held the doves. One flapped its wings; the other didn't seem to be moving.

Grace and Riley each took a bird, and then on the cue from the officiant, they opened the cages at the same time. Neither bird flew away, though, preferring to stay in their cozy cages. After some prompting, one dove launched from its cage into the sky in a burst of feathers.

Everyone clapped, but the applause ended as soon as it began. The poor dove had barely escaped before a hawk swooped down, snagged the dove, and flew away with it in its talons. Worse, the officiant yelled, "Oh shit!" straight into his mic.

The guests went silent. You could hear a pin drop.

I caught Anna's eye. She was pale as a ghost, her hand over her mouth. But in a bit of quick thinking, she took the second dove from Riley, closing the cage door before it, too, could become a hawk's lunch.

~

A HALF HOUR later during cocktail hour, I found Anna again. She was slugging champagne like it was Gatorade. Fortunately, though, the food and booze seemed to be enough to help everyone else forget the earlier spectacle.

"Where'd you put the second dove?" I asked her.

"Inside the bride's dressing room. There's AC in there. I don't want the poor thing to die, too." Anna sighed. "I told them the dove release was a bad idea."

"Really?"

"Yes, really. At first Grace wanted to release hundreds of butterflies, but I've seen that go wrong more than once. You order a box of butterflies and end up with a box of *dead* butterflies that don't fly. Or worse, they're half-alive and end up falling on your guests' heads."

I couldn't restrain my laughter now. "I would've paid money to see that."

"I told her that a dove release could be bad news, but the bride insisted." Anna shrugged. "At least they weren't both eaten."

"I'm sure the other dove is very grateful," I said solemnly.

Anna finished her glass of champagne before flagging down a waiter who carried a tray of appetizers. "God, I'm starving. Are these vegan? Whatever, I don't even care."

Anna wolfed down three apps, snagging another glass of wine. "So, why are you here?" she asked me.

We'd wandered away from most of the guests, finding a little quiet and shade under a eucalyptus tree. "Riley's my cousin," I said. I shot her a look. "And *you're* here. How is it that you're at every wedding in LA?"

"I have a lot of friends."

"I find that hard to believe."

"I'm not nearly drunk enough to listen to you insult me."

I grinned. I liked this version of Anna Dyer. With a few drinks in her, she was snarkier. Even better, she didn't seem to notice that her gown was riding up her thighs or that one of her straps had fallen down her arm already.

"I'm not trying to insult you," I said demurely, "but you don't seem like the type of woman to collect friends."

"How do you know what type of woman I am? What does that even mean?"

"I mean, some people collect friends. Alejo is like that. He's so fucking friendly that everybody is his friend. I swear he invited his mailman to Thanksgiving last year."

"So you're saying I'm not friendly?" Anna's lips twitched.

"You're not. . ." I didn't know where I was going with this conversation, besides digging my grave further. "Never mind. I'm just talking bullshit."

"Oh, I already knew that. But I'm intrigued anyway. I mean, during our last meeting, you didn't seem all that impressed with me, or with my business."

I could hear the edge in her voice. "My feelings about weddings have nothing to do with my feelings about you."

"So you have feelings for me?" she joked.

That grave of mine was going deeper than six feet. It was going straight to the core of the earth. "You know what? I think I heard that the reception is starting," I lied.

Anna was apparently feeling kind enough that she didn't call me out on my lie. Besides, the bride needed her for something dress-related, so I didn't speak to Anna again until the dancing began.

When the DJ started playing "The Electric Slide," I wanted to bolt. Who in their right mind enjoyed this cheesy shit? But based on the guests' reaction, you'd think the DJ had told them they'd all won a million dollars, they were that excited.

The woman next to me, a pretty blonde, had been giving me eyes the entire time during dinner. She was also alone. Feeling chivalrous, I asked her to dance. I also couldn't remember her name. Denise? Dana? It started with a D, that much I was certain.

Denise-Dana was handsy. Too handsy. I had to move her hands off my ass three times, to the point that I was tempted to give her a good tit-squeeze in revenge.

"I think we're the only singles here," Denise-Dana said, batting her fake eyelashes. She was batting them so quickly that I was afraid that the lashes would take off and fly away.

"Are we?" I said.

"Which means we should stick together. I almost didn't come, you know. I broke up with my boyfriend a month ago, but I'd already RSVP'd. But I'm glad I came." Denise-Dana shot me a coy smile.

I groaned inwardly. I didn't mind women coming on to me. What straight man did? But Denise-Dana had no subtlety. It was all "grab his ass" and nothing in between.

Was this what it was like for women? Because it was definitely obnoxious, being treated like a piece of meat.

"May I cut in?" Anna said.

Before Denise-Dana could say yes, I was taking Anna's hand and leading her away.

"Thank you," I muttered, shaking my head.

"You looked a little like a deer in headlights." Anna patted my arm.

To my horror, the next song was a slow song. Which meant swaying with Anna like middle schoolers.

"I'm not used to women acting like that," I admitted.

"Really? I don't believe you."

I fake-gasped. "Are you complimenting me?"

"You have hair, you're tall, you bathe—I assume—regularly. That makes you a catch, believe me."

"Well, now you're making me blush." My voice dripped with sarcasm. "And here I thought you were attracted to me."

To my amusement, Anna's cheeks were the ones turning red now. I twirled her, and she came back with even redder cheeks. She also wouldn't look me in the eye.

Either she thought I was hot, or she'd had too much to drink. Maybe a little bit of both.

"Now you're just digging for compliments," she complained.

"Only because I know you hate giving them to me."

"I have nothing against you personally. Not sure where you got that from."

I shrugged. "And I have nothing against you. So we're on the same page there."

She gazed up at me, her lashes shading her eyes, making

her seem almost demure. Which was hilarious, because there wasn't a demure bone in this woman's body.

It didn't help that her body kept pressing closer and closer to mine. I could feel her curves, feel the warmth of her skin under my hands. Every time she moved, I could smell a bit of lemon.

My cock stirred. I forced myself to think of glaciers, ice floes, cold showers—

"You look like you're going to have a stroke," Anna said.

I barked out a laugh. "That's just my face. So much for finding me attractive."

She wrinkled her nose, which was obnoxiously adorable. I also couldn't help but notice that she had freckles on her nose and a few on her chest and shoulders. It made me wonder where else she had a smattering of freckles.

"How long have you known Grace?" I asked, my voice hoarse.

Anna blinked. "Who?"

"Um, the bride. That's her name, right? Shit, did I write the wrong name down on their card—"

"Sorry, sorry, you're right. Her name is Grace. Brain fart." Anna laughed, but it sounded strained.

"So you must be good friends to be her maid of honor."

"She knew I'd do a good job," was Anna's odd answer.

I was about to ask her what she meant when the song changed to another fast one. And before I could react, Anna was walking away without so much as a goodbye.

I frowned. What the hell had that been about?

I spent another hour at the reception, eating and avoiding Denise-Dana. Fortunately for me, she managed to find the one other single male and was now stalking him. I breathed a sigh of relief when I saw her lead her latest prey to the dance floor.

After saying goodbye to Riley, I went in search of Grace. Riley pointed me toward a back hallway, indicating that his new wife had wandered in that direction.

I stopped when I heard a woman crying. Then I heard Anna's voice saying, "It wasn't that bad."

"A fucking *hawk* killed one of the doves! Everybody's going to remember that."

"No, they won't. It was just an unfortunate blip—"

"You said you were the best in the business."

I winced inwardly. I glanced around the corner, confirming that it was Grace who was the one crying.

"I'm good at what I do," replied Anna. "I also warned you guys that releasing animals was risky." Her voice was calm.

Grace hiccupped. "I don't care. I don't want to talk to you. I'm tired of this."

"I'm sorry you're unhappy. It was a beautiful wedding. I'm not just saying that to make you feel better."

"You should've made Riley understand about the doves. I told him it was a dumb idea, but he wanted to do it anyway. I guess even the best bridesmaid in the business isn't on her A game all the time."

As I drove to the nearby hotel to turn in for the night, I wondered what that entire thing had been about. "Best bridesmaid in the business"?

So had Anna also been the wedding planner? She hadn't mentioned that. Then again, why would she? It wasn't like we were friends. We were acquaintances at most —which was exactly how things should stay.

CHAPTER SIX

ANNA

I arrived at the hotel, changed into my pajamas, completely exhausted. Which meant that I ended up staring at the ceiling, my mind whirling, completely unable to sleep. It didn't help that my stomach was rumbling. Apparently I hadn't eaten as many appetizers as I'd thought.

I pulled on a sweatshirt and went downstairs to the hotel bar. It was past midnight, and there were all of three people sitting at the bar. Based on their clothing, they'd also come from a wedding.

When I spotted Rowan sitting at a booth in the corner by himself, I didn't react quickly enough to avoid his gaze. And when he motioned me to sit with him, I sighed inwardly. I wasn't going to get out of this one, apparently.

He was drinking whiskey or brandy or whatever manly liquor guys like him preferred. He was still wearing his suit sans jacket, the collar unbuttoned and the tie loosened. He looked rumpled—and delicious. In the low lighting of the bar and the privacy of the booth, I could almost imagine we were the only two people in existence.

It was too late when I remembered I was wearing pajama shorts with ducks on them. My sweatshirt had seen better days. Was that a grease stain on the front? Hopefully it was too dim for Rowan to notice.

"Did you not want a drink?" asked Rowan.

"I ordered some food. I'm hungry."

He grinned lazily. "I've never met a woman who eats as much as you do." Probably realizing what he just said, he grimaced. "I mean, shit, I didn't mean that—"

I laughed at his pained expression. "I like food. I can't deny it."

"I didn't mean to imply that you were fat."

I had to chew on the inside of my cheek to keep from laughing harder. "Are you saying that it's a bad thing to be fat?"

He looked like he wanted to dive under the table. "No. I mean, you aren't. Just in case you were afraid you were."

I really should've taken pity on the poor man, but then my burger and fries arrived. I was too hungry to put him out of his misery in that moment.

I took a large bite of my burger. "So, now that you've called me a glutton and a fatty—"

"I never said *that*—"

"How are you? FYI, you have a very long nose hair hanging from your right nostril."

Rowan checked the offending nostril. Then he glared at me, realizing he'd been played.

"I deserved that," he said wryly.

I grinned and popped a fry into my mouth. "Oh yeah, you did."

"You know, I'm usually much better around women. Tonight was an off night."

"You mean you're usually smooth and charming? I have a hard time believing that."

His eyes sparkled. To my surprise, I felt his hand grazing my thigh: the touch was fleeting, but it made my entire body tingle.

Worse, he leaned forward and said in a rough voice, "You looked gorgeous tonight."

Was he serious or just playing with me? I didn't have the guts to ask. "Thanks," I croaked.

"But I wanted to take your hair down all evening, see it tumble down your shoulders, sift my fingers through it as we danced."

I couldn't breathe. Then Rowan sat back and grinned, like a cat that'd caught the canary.

I kicked him underneath the table. "Jesus, you nearly gave me a heart attack," I complained.

"I can put on the charm if I really want to."

"Congrats. I'm sure your mother is very proud."

"My mom is dead."

I blushed. "Crap, I'm sorry—"

He grinned again. "Gotcha."

I kicked him, this time making him wince. "You're such an asshole! I can't believe I felt sorry for you earlier when that chick was about to deep-throat you on the dance floor."

Rowan choked on his drink. "Christ, Anna!"

"She was all up in your business."

He shot me a strange look. "Were you jealous?"

"Jealous!" I barked out a laugh, which I was embarrassed to realize sounded like a seal. "No fucking way. I just felt sorry for you. Or for her. Maybe both."

"You sounded jealous. Like you wanted to deep-throat me on the dance floor."

Now I was the one choking. It got to the point that I had to finish off my water while Rowan went to get me another glass for good measure.

My eyes were watering, my nose was running, and sweat had broken out on my forehead.

"You okay?" asked Rowan. Now he sounded genuinely concerned.

"Fine, fine. It's my fault bringing up deep-throating."

"Say it any louder and we're going to have people asking me if I'm trying to hire you for the night."

"Oh, you couldn't afford me." I batted my eyelashes. "I mean, did you see what I'm wearing? I'm very high-class. Duck pajamas and all."

"Those tiny shorts? That's just easy access."

I rolled my eyes, even though my heart started pounding. I still couldn't tell if he was genuinely flirting with me or if he was just playing around. Then again, I might just have lost oxygen to my brain after nearly choking on a fry.

"I am surprised you're still awake," said Rowan.

"I told you: I was hungry."

"Planning a wedding must be tiring. Aren't you exhausted?"

"I was the maid of honor, not the planner."

He gave me a strange look. "Really?"

It wasn't that my business as being a bridesmaid-for-hire was a secret, per se. But I preferred to keep that knowledge on the down-low, mostly for the brides. Finding out that the bride hired someone to play her friend and bridesmaid was a bit gauche to most people.

And I had a feeling that Rowan, of all people, definitely wouldn't understand. He thought weddings were pointless, after all.

"Yes, really. I don't plan every wedding I attend. Thank God. I'd have died of exhaustion long ago if that were the case," I said.

"You never said how you knew the bride."

"We met in college," I lied. "We'd recently reconnected, and having me as maid of honor made things easier so she didn't have to choose between her many female cousins."

It was one of the standard stories I fed people who asked questions, with the details changed as necessary. And up to this point, no one had ever questioned those stories.

"You'd recently reconnected to the point that she asked you to be her maid of honor?" Rowan looked skeptical. "I thought that was a big deal."

"Not for every bride."

"Yet Grace seemed to expect a whole lot from you tonight."

I stared at him. "You were eavesdropping? Seriously?"

"It wasn't on purpose." He shrugged, not at all ashamed.

I felt a mixture of outrage and embarrassment that Rowan had overheard Grace chewing me out. Sure, I'd warned her and Riley multiple times about releasing doves, but had they listened? Nope. And Grace, upset with what had happened, had taken it out on me.

It had sucked. It was the one aspect of this job that I

hated, when the bride or groom would get upset with me even though I'd done my best to give them good advice. There were always so many expectations when it came to weddings that any snafus felt like absolute catastrophes. And the snafu today had definitely been in the top five in all the weddings I'd been involved in.

"Grace kept saying you were the 'best in the business,'" Rowan was saying. "But you were just her maid of honor, right?"

I rolled my eyes. "You know what? Fine. She hired me to be her maid of honor. I'm a bridesmaid-for-hire, along with being a wedding planner. Is that what you wanted to hear? That she paid me to plan her bachelorette party and to fix her dress and veil for all of her pictures?"

Rowan looked smug. "I knew it."

"It's hardly a smoking gun. It's not illegal, for God's sake."

"No, but you getting paid to act like someone's friend is. . ." He shook his head. "Shady."

"Wow." I gaped at him. "You have some nerve to act like you're so high and mighty? Like I'm doing something immoral? Come on. Get off your high horse. You just hate weddings because you hate love, or whatever boring reason you have to think they're stupid."

"You sound defensive."

I wanted to rip his eyes out. Instead, I stood up and said, "This conversation is over. I didn't come down here to be insulted."

"Anna! Anna, come on—"

I was faster than I looked. By the time Rowan caught up

with me, I was already in the elevator. I made a point to press the *close door* button just as he was about to get on.

"Seriously?" I heard him say as the doors closed in his face.

But I'd been so set on not letting him on the elevator that I hadn't actually chosen my floor. So the doors eventually reopened to his stupid, smiling, smug face.

"We meet again," he drawled. He stepped inside the elevator.

I ignored him. I pressed the number five and crossed my arms, refusing to look at him.

He got off on the fifth floor with me. I whirled on him, snarling, "Will you stop following me?"

That smug grin hadn't left his face. "I'm on this floor, actually." He flashed the envelope containing his hotel keys, where the number 515 was scrawled in pen.

"God, will this nightmare never end?" I said with a groan.

Of course, because the universe apparently had it out for me, my room was only three doors away from his. This meant he followed me down one hallway, then another, neither of us saying a word.

When I got to my door, I slid the keycard into the lock too quickly. The red light flashed. I tried again, only to nearly have a heart attack when Rowan came up behind me, his body caging me in.

"I didn't mean to insult you," he said, his mouth dangerously close to my ear. "I just don't get why anyone would pay for that."

"It's fine."

"You don't sound like you think it's fine."

I whirled around. "Look, you and I are never going to agree on a lot of things. But the moment you insult my integrity is when you take it a step too far."

He at least had the grace to look abashed. "Anna, I'm sorry."

I didn't want to forgive him. I wanted to stew in my anger. It was easier to be angry with him, because then I could avoid thinking about how I'd like to feel about him.

"Will you forgive me?" he asked.

"I'll consider it."

He leaned closer. He smelled of whiskey, and I was unfortunately eye level with his open collar, where a triangle of tanned skin peered through.

"Come on," he cajoled, "let's be friends again."

"We've never been friends."

"I'd like to be friends."

My heart seized. My entire body felt aflame. I had the stupidest desire to lick his throat, feel his Adam's apple bob under my tongue.

"Anna." He touched my cheek. "Look at me."

I looked at him.

"I'm sorry."

I licked my lips. "Okay," I breathed.

I waited for him to do something. Anything. Kiss me, embrace me, even toss me aside. The tension became so great that I felt like I was going to lose my mind.

Instead, he stepped back. The thread of tension snapped, giving me whiplash.

"Have a good night," he said. He looked so unruffled that I was irritated. Here I was, my body on fire, and he didn't seem to care or notice. Was the man made of stone?

And why flirt with me all evening and then go cold all of a sudden? My annoyance flared.

"You sure you don't want to come inside my room, after basically mauling me?" I asked, sarcasm dripping from my voice.

His jaw tightened; his smile was strained now. "Oh, I definitely can't afford your fee," was his cold reply before he walked away.

CHAPTER SEVEN

ANNA

Melanie wrinkled her nose. "I can't believe you're seriously working with my ex-boyfriend."

"It's not by choice, believe me."

Melanie swirled her wine, considering. We hadn't seen each other in two weeks—I'd been busy with work, she'd been busy chasing after a new guy—and we had a lot to update each other on.

"There were a lot of red flags when we were dating, but he was so hot I ignored them." Melanie shrugged. "And the sex wasn't bad, either. That might've been why I kept Rowan around for so long."

I winced inwardly. I did not want to know the details of Melanie and Rowan sleeping together. And I absolutely could not tell Melanie that, despite his asshole behavior, I was stupidly attracted to Rowan anyway.

"You guys were pretty young," I hedged.

"I mean, we weren't in high school, but sometimes it felt like we were. I remember we got into this insane fight one night. I threw a mug at his head, and he just went cold. He wouldn't talk to me for a week, no matter how much I apologized. I'd go over to his place and he'd just refuse to open the door."

"You never told me that," I said, surprised.

"It was a long time ago. I think I was embarrassed to talk about it. Everyone thought we were the cutest couple, and having people know that was a complete lie? No, thanks. I didn't need that in my life."

I bit my tongue when I wanted to remark that Melanie tended to care way too much about what other people thought. She also tended to care deeply about her image, to the point that she'd tie herself up in knots if she caught a whiff of someone not liking her. I'd never understood it. When I'd pointed that out once, she'd gotten so angry at me that I'd been worried that our friendship was over.

"Rowan, though, he was addictive," Melanie was saying. "Like I couldn't just let him go. I kept wanting to go back. And he'd draw me again, and we'd be happy for a while, and then something would blow up. Rinse, repeat. It was exhausting. It didn't help that any time I mentioned being committed, he'd change the subject."

Melanie smiled wryly. "I'm always surprised that you keep having people come to you to get married. I feel like every guy in LA has commitment issues."

"Oh, they still have commitment issues," I said with a laugh. "You should see some of the grooms on the day of the wedding. Just some, though. Most of them genuinely want to get married."

"Where does a girl find a guy like that?" Melanie sighed. "Asking for a friend, you know."

"You and me both, sister."

Melanie went on to tell me about the latest guy she'd hooked up with, some singer she'd met at a festival. He was apparently amazing in bed, had an adorable dog, and was passionate about the environment.

He also lived with his mom.

"Oh, Mel," I said, shaking my head. "Please tell me it's not what it sounds like."

"He's looking for a place. It's hard to find something affordable."

"You mean he lives in his mom's basement and has no reason to move out any time soon. Please tell me she doesn't do his laundry, clean his room, make him dinner. . ."

Melanie just drank her wine and refused to answer.

"You know you can do better than that," I pointed out.

"Sure, but sometimes that's too much work. I hate to be alone. You know that. I'm not like you. You're happy being single."

That night, lying in bed by myself, I considered Melanie's remark. Was I happy being single? For the most part, yes. There were times when I wished I wasn't alone. It'd be nice to come home to somebody in the evening. It'd be nice to have somebody to go on vacations with, to cook for, to pass through life with.

It'd also be nice to have a man who loved me and *wanted* me. Growing up, that hadn't seemed a monumental task to accomplish, but as I'd gotten older, finding that man seemed more and more difficult. If he didn't have commitment issues, he was immature. Or he straight-up was disrespectful to women. I wasn't so desperate for a man that I'd let myself be treated badly.

I was about to turn off the light when I received a text. It was from Rowan.

Let's get drinks soon. I'll pay.

I stared at the message. Had he just asked me out on a date? Or was this strictly business?

Are you hitting on me, Caldwell? I replied.

Only if you want me to be.

Okay. . .

We need to talk, he replied.

Oh, great. Talk. I wasn't interested in having another argument with Rowan Caldwell, but I also knew he was right. If we were going to work together to plan Emily and Alejo's wedding, we'd have to be civil with one another. We had an entire year where we'd have to interact with each other.

I agreed to meet Rowan Wednesday evening at a new tapas place in Glendale. Although Glendale was a farther drive for Rowan than for me in nearby Pasadena, he'd been firm on the location.

Then I proceeded to lay awake all night, wondering if this was actually going to be a date.

I DECIDED to wear a dress that was a good cross between business and cocktail wear. I spent way too much time trying to decide what to wear, all the while knowing that I was not actually going on a date.

Besides, even if he did ask you out, you can't date Melanie's ex-boyfriend.

Melanie would never, ever forgive me. She was loyal, but

she was also the type of person to hold a grudge. She'd go to her deathbed telling people that her best friend had betrayed her. Her ghost would probably haunt me, too.

When I got to the restaurant, I found Rowan sitting down already, a stack of envelopes on the table. He barely glanced at me as I sat down across from him.

"Are you attending any of these weddings?" He handed me the stack.

"Nice to see you, too," I said sarcastically.

"Just look through those. Do you want a drink?"

After ordering one of the most expensive drinks on the menu—Rowan had said he was paying—I looked through the stack. They were all wedding invitations, I realized.

"You're going to all of these weddings?" I asked.

"Probably. Were you invited?"

"All but one, actually. I don't know this couple." I held up the envelope that had skulls in the corner.

Rowan's lips quirked. "It's a Halloween wedding. Apparently they want everyone to wear costumes, too."

"I might have to crash that one anyway."

"Really?"

"Why do you sound so surprised?"

He shrugged. "I guess I would've assumed that a wedding fanatic like you would hate the idea of a Halloween wedding."

"Geez, you really think I'm a stick-in-the-mud, don't you? I can assure you that I didn't have a stroke the first time a bride wanted to wear ivory instead of white." I leaned forward, lowering my voice to a whisper. "I've even had brides wear *black*. One wore red. Another wore a literal rainbow gown."

"And you survived that?" Rowan placed his hand over his heart in mock horror. "I don't believe it."

"Okay, Mister Wedding, why did you ask me out again? Because if this is your idea of a date, it's a fucking weird one."

His lips quirked, but his expression quickly turned somber. "First off, I wanted to apologize for the other night. I was out of line."

I stared at Rowan in genuine shock. I looked around, as if I'd spot hidden cameras somewhere. "Now I'm extra confused," I confessed.

"Secondly, I asked you here because I wanted to hear your thoughts on an idea I have."

"If you're asking me to join your MLM, I'm not interested in buying your essential oils, please and thank you."

He barely cracked a smile. "Since we're both going to all these weddings, I thought we'd go together."

"Like, carpool? That's very environmentally friendly of you, Mr. Caldwell. Although I have to confess, I totally use the express lanes even when it's just me in the car."

"Anna." Rowan crossed his arms. "Are you being deliberately obtuse?"

I blinked. "No. . .?"

He rolled his eyes. I had to restrain the urge to kick him under the table.

"I want you to be my plus-one. That's what I'm asking you. Do you get it now?" he said.

"I have to say, this date just keeps getting weirder."

He looked pained. "If you're just going to make jokes all night—"

I held up a hand. "Sorry, sorry. I'm just confused. Why

do you need a plus-one? Can't we just hang out at the wedding that we're both invited to?"

"I want you to be my plus-one because I'm tired of people asking why I'm there alone. And I have a feeling you're tired of it, too."

"So you want me to be your date because you're embarrassed about being single?" I tapped my chin. "How is that my problem?"

"It's not. But we both have a problem that we could solve. Together. I want to be left alone; you want to avoid people thinking you're a spinster. It makes perfect sense."

I laughed, but it came out more like a choking noise. "Oh my God! Are you negging me to go on dates with you? Rowan, I'm flattered, but I'm sure we'll both be okay attending weddings as single people. Besides, since I'm in the wedding party of two of those weddings, it's not like I'm going to be shunted to a table in the back with the other spinsters.

"Besides, this isn't the nineteenth century. Nobody cares if I'm a *spinster*. Jesus Christ on a cracker."

Rowan was gritting his teeth. I had to admit, him looking pained and frustrated was kind of turning me on. Or maybe it was because in this instance, I had all the power.

"I shouldn't have called you that," he admitted. "Sorry."

I waved a hand. "At this point, it's the least offensive thing you've said to me."

"Aren't you tired of people asking you why you're alone? When you're getting married? Because I am. When I was in my twenties, nobody gave a shit about 'settling down.' Now,

I can't shake a stick without a woman trying to drag me to the altar," said Rowan.

I snort-laughed. "I'm struggling to see, once again, how that's my problem."

He leaned forward, his eyes gleaming. "What if I promised that I could hook you up with one of the biggest advertisers in the city. Somebody who could take your business to the next level, get you A-list clients."

I had to admit, my curiosity was piqued. "Go on."

"I used to work at the same tech firm as Alejo. One of the guys who we started with is the CEO of AppVille. If I called in a favor, he'd do it, no questions asked."

Damn Rowan. That was a delicious carrot he was dangling in front of me.

"This seems very one-sided. I pose as your girlfriend a few times, and I get access to the CEO of AppVille? I still don't get what's in it for you," I said.

Rowan shrugged. "Does it matter? Those are my terms."

I considered him. It didn't help that his collar was unbuttoned or that it looked like he'd been running his fingers through his hair all evening. I wanted to grab him by the collar and kiss him, then unbutton his shirt the rest of the way to admire his sculpted pecs, his perfectly delineated abs. . .

Rowan snapped his fingers in front of my face. "Anna. Are you listening?"

I shoved his hand away. "Don't snap at me like I'm a dog. At least give me a treat first, sheesh."

"So are you saying yes or no?" He glanced at his watch. "I have to be somewhere."

"Geez, no pressure or anything." I narrowed my eyes at him as a thought occurred to me. "If I'm posing as your girlfriend, that means we're going to have to act like a couple. Touching, hugging, maybe even kissing. Are you expecting me to have sex with you? Because that's a hard no."

He laughed. Tipped his head back, opened his mouth, and guffawed until he had tears in his eyes.

Well, that told me everything I needed to know about how much he wanted to sleep with me.

"God," he was saying, still laughing, "you say the craziest shit."

"You didn't answer my question."

"No, Anna Dyer, I'm not expecting us to have sex to prove that our relationship is real."

My feathers were ruffled. It was stupid, and it annoyed me that I cared. I finished off my drink in one long swallow.

"Well, if that's the case, then you have a deal." I stuck out my hand, and a moment later, Rowan shook it.

Rowan walked me out to my car. I was suddenly nervous, and when he touched the small of my back, I jumped.

"Why are you mad?" he asked, his breath warm against my face.

"I'm not mad."

"If you want to sleep with me that badly, you just say the word." His hand, damn him, trailed down my spine until it rested right above my ass.

I had to close my eyes and take a deep breath. "I don't think of you that way," I lied.

His hand moved back up, until he cupped the nape of my neck. Then he turned me toward him and kissed me.

The kiss wasn't polite. It wasn't sweet, either. He kissed me hard, plunging his tongue into my mouth, forcing me to grip his shoulders so I didn't collapse at his feet. Explosions rocked my body. Fireworks burst inside my eyelids.

And then, it was over.

"Liar," he said, looking smug and way too pleased with himself.

"What?"

"You want me so bad."

My eyes widened. "Oh my God—"

"I bet if I reached under your dress and inside your panties, I'd find you dripping." His heated words made me shiver. "Tell me I'm wrong."

My pussy was pulsing, and I couldn't deny his assertion. It didn't help that the thought of him fingering me made me nearly moan aloud.

"You suck," was all I could manage. I turned to unlock my door, struggling for a moment and making Rowan laugh.

"Good night, Anna," he said. "Go home and rub one out with me in mind, won't you?"

I just gave him the middle finger and drove off.

CHAPTER EIGHT

ROWAN

It started raining the moment I stepped outside. Normally, I'd be happy to see it raining. It wasn't exactly a common occurrence in a place like Pasadena, and it meant that perhaps this year, fire season might not be terrible for once.

But when the rain turned to a downpour, I grimly realized that I was going to be late to pick Anna up. My driveway had become a muddy mess, the gravel washing away down the hill that led to my house and farm. It'd been so long since it'd rained that it was as if the earth itself didn't know how to cope. Fortunately, though, the road looked okay. It was just my driveway that was a mess.

I got into my truck, revving the engine, but my tires just squealed in protest.

"Fuck," I said, getting out and stamping through the mud. Looking at my watch, I knew that I'd be late now.

I didn't have time to change out of my wedding clothes, either. I grabbed a few wooden boards from the nearby barn, tromping through the mud and not caring that my pants were getting soaked. I shoved the boards under the back tires and climbed back inside the truck.

"Come on, come on," I muttered as I reversed onto the boards. "Just get me out of here onto the gravel."

I felt the tires dig in, but by some miracle I managed to get the truck onto the road. I blew out a breath of relief.

I knew I was being a complete idiot. It wasn't like I was trying to get somewhere because of an emergency. But I'd been the one to suggest Anna be my plus-one for all these upcoming weddings, and the last thing I wanted was for her to think I was getting cold feet.

My phone buzzed in my pocket. It buzzed a second and then a third time. I played the voicemail, groaning as I listened.

"Hey, Rowan, just making sure you didn't forget that you were supposed to pick me up, well, now," Anna said. "And the thing is, my car is in the shop, so it's either your car or I get an Uber. Call me, okay?"

Traffic slowed to its usual standstill as I pulled my phone out of my pocket. I shot Anna a quick text, confirming that I was on my way.

I arrived twenty minutes late. When Anna stepped out of her house and saw me, her jaw dropped.

"What the hell happened?" she demanded.

I looked down and realized that I was covered in mud. My pants, my shoes, and my jacket. There were even splatters of mud on my face.

"Come on, I have a suit inside you can borrow. You can't go to the wedding like that," said Anna, ushering me inside.

"We're gonna be late," I replied.

"Knowing this couple, they're probably running late anyway. Did you decide to take up mud wrestling in your spare time? And don't take another step inside before taking off your shoes. You are not tracking mud everywhere."

I obeyed, feeling like a kid getting scolded.

Anna's house was a tiny little bungalow with stucco walls and a flat roof that was so common in the area. All her windows were open, letting in the smell of rain waft indoors. She had a fireplace framed in colorful tiles, along with wicker furniture that seemed more suitable for a porch.

Her place was filled with stuff. Her dining room table was covered in ribbons, tape, scissors, glitter, invitations, and bags and bags of stuff that I couldn't begin to name. Dresses hung from doorframes. There was even an entire arch framing her front window that had faux florals already on it.

"Come on." Anna gestured toward the back of the house. "Here, take off your clothes and clean up. I'll get the suit for you."

"You just have entire suits lying around your house?"

"Of course I do. And I'm pretty sure I have one that'll fit you, although it might be a tad too short. You're pretty tall."

That remark made me grin. "So you've noticed."

"You're covered in mud, Rowan. Now is not the time to flirt."

I watched Anna walk away, her pert ass making my mouth water. It didn't help that she was wearing a dress that left little to the imagination.

Get it together, I told myself sharply. Now was not the time to get a hard-on.

I stripped out of my clothes down to my boxers before wiping myself down as best I could.

Anna knocked on the bathroom door. "Are you clean?"

I opened the door wide, not caring if she saw me in only my boxers. She blushed, which just made me chuckle.

"Please tell me you didn't get mud all over my bathroom." She looked over my shoulder. "You know what? Never mind. I don't want to know."

"Probably wise," I replied solemnly.

I dressed quickly, impressed that Anna had correctly guessed my size. The jacket was a bit too short, but not enough for anyone to notice. I combed my hair, wiped up any mud left behind, and tossed the dirty washcloth into a nearby hamper.

I found Anna in her living room, pacing. "Oh, you look good," she said, looking surprised.

I gave her a little twirl. "Do I meet your expectations?"

She came closer to straighten my tie. She brushed a few bits of lint from the jacket before stepping back and assessing me.

I could see the desire in her eyes. It was the same look she'd given me when I'd kissed her two weeks ago.

Just the thought of how she'd felt in my arms, the way she'd gasped my name, made my cock awaken. I was suddenly grateful that the pants were a little big in the waist.

"Um, okay. Shoes. Hopefully these fit." Anna shoved a pair into my hands, not looking me in the eye. "Then we should go."

I sat down and put on the shoes, watching her out of the corner of my eye. Anna kept wringing her hands, her cheeks flushed.

"Is this going to be awkward from now on?" I asked, getting up.

Her gaze flew to mine. "Huh?"

"Since I kissed you that night. Because I don't feel awkward about it."

A dark cloud passed over her expression. "Um, of course not. Come on, let's get going before traffic gets bad."

"It's LA. The traffic is always bad," I pointed out.

THE WEDDING WAS about what you'd expect: there was a ceremony, then there was a reception. There were vows, bouquets, toasts that lasted way too long, awkward dancing, and very dry chicken. The bride was a coworker from years back, while Anna knew the groom from high school.

It was a huge wedding, with upwards of three hundred people. Neither Anna nor I had a moment to even say hello to the bride and groom.

It was getting close to ten p.m., the reception already winding down, when I bent down to whisper in Anna's ear, "Wanna get out of this place?"

"God, yes. I'm *starving*."

I laughed. We quickly decided to get chicken and waffles, and we were both so hungry that we barely spoke until we'd had our fill.

The rain had cleared up, the night cool and clear. Traffic buzzed along the 210, the sound of engines revving and horns honking giving the night a very LA-sounding soundtrack.

"I feel so much better," Anna said with a sigh. She put her head down on the table. "I could fall asleep right here."

"It's not even midnight. Are you already falling asleep on me, Dyer?"

She didn't even pick up her head to say, "Food coma. Can't talk."

I was strangely energized. I wanted to go drinking, go dancing, go do something. Which was completely unlike me. I preferred to keep to myself most nights. I hadn't partied hard since my early twenties.

"Come on, the night is young," I said, grabbing Anna by her arm.

She protested, but when I managed to find a spot on the street in front of a newly opened bar/arcade that I'd heard Alejo raving about, she perked up.

The place was packed. It was filled with arcade games from the eighties and nineties. There was also Skee-Ball, pinball machines, air hockey, and a tournament where you could play N64 games like *Mario Kart 64*.

"You like video games?" asked Anna.

"Not really."

"So you brought me to an arcade, why?"

I didn't have an answer to that. Instead, I grunted something and went to get us both drinks.

Anna, I came to find out, was crazy competitive. When I beat her at air hockey, she nearly tackled me, yelling that I'd cheated on that last turn.

"How can you cheat at air hockey?" I was laughing as she was trying to take my disc away. "You lost!"

"Another!" Anna's jaw was clenched. "And I'm going to kick your ass, Caldwell."

She didn't kick my ass, which only enraged her further. I made sure to provide her with more drinks until her competitiveness was somewhat less threatening. I didn't really need Anna to rip off my balls because she'd lost a game of Skee-Ball, thank you very much.

Anna was tipsy and red-faced when she began playing an old shooter game, holding the plastic rifle on her shoulder. But when she kept missing the targets, I went behind her and helped her hold the rifle steady.

"You have to aim to the right of the target," I said into her ear. "I played this game when I was a kid."

"That makes zero sense," she groused.

"Try it."

She did, which only made her frown more. At that moment, I knew I should step away from her, but I found myself not wanting to let her go.

My hands spanned her waist, and I was so close that I could kiss her ear. It didn't help that she was breathing hard, her luscious tits practically bursting from her dress.

I couldn't help myself: I licked her ear, ever so slightly. She jerked in surprise. She turned her head to look at me, her eyes wide, her pupils blown wide.

"Rowan," she whispered.

"I lied." My voice was rough. "About not giving a shit about that kiss. I lied."

She said nothing, but I could see her blush growing deeper.

"I want to kiss you again. I want to rip off your panties and find out how pink and sweet your pussy is. And then I want to plunge my cock deep inside you."

Anna was breathing so hard that I was slightly afraid she'd hyperventilate.

"We can't," she said, sounding not remotely convinced.

"Why? Are you dating somebody else?" Jealousy made my tone sharp.

She shook her head. "No, but you're dating someone. I mean, you dated someone. Melanie. She's my best friend."

"Seriously? We broke up years ago."

Anna put distance between us, returning the plastic rifle to its holder. "What does that matter? You guys were in a relationship. I can't do that to Melanie. She'd never forgive me."

I wanted to tear my hair out. I also wanted to throw Anna over my shoulder like some fucking caveman, carry her off, and have my way with her. And here my ex-girlfriend was, trying to keep us apart? Fuck that shit.

"She's a big girl," I said. "She can deal with it. It's not like we were married with five kids. We didn't even date for a year."

Anna just kept shaking her head. "I can't. I just can't. You can't convince me. There's no use in trying to argue your way into getting me to change my mind."

When she lifted her stubborn, gorgeous, frustrating chin, I knew she was right. I couldn't use logic here. This entire thing was based on emotion and the strange loyalty between female friends.

I drove Anna home in silence. She stared out the window the entire time, barely even looking at me when I asked her for directions since I'd only been to her house once now. She seemed pensive. Even a little sad.

When I parked in front of her house, I waited. I didn't

know why, since I knew she wasn't going to suddenly change her mind and invite me in.

"We probably should never have agreed to be each other's plus-ones," Anna said suddenly.

I raised an eyebrow. "Do you want to call it off? Because I can assure you, I won't manhandle you if you want me to leave you alone."

"That's the thing. I don't want you to leave me alone. I just know that I *should* want that."

I growled. I pulled her close, kissing her with a fervor that showed her how much I hated what she'd just said.

"Who gives a fuck about what you should do?" I was the one breathing hard now. "We wouldn't be doing anything wrong."

"But I'd feel like I was doing something wrong." Anna sighed. "That's the problem. I'm not willing to destroy my friendship just to have okay sex a few times."

"'Okay sex'? Darling, when you're with me, sex would be anything but okay." I traced a finger down her throat until it reached her cleavage. I dipped inside her dress, almost brushing against her hardened nipples. "I'd fuck your brains out, and you know it."

She licked her lips, which made my cock come to attention once again. "Oh, I know it. That's why it scares me."

CHAPTER NINE

ANNA

I didn't want to get out of Rowan's car. I wished I weren't so responsible. Wouldn't it just be easier to throw caution to the wind and damn the consequences?

"I should get my clothes," said Rowan suddenly.

Suddenly, the idea of Rowan entering my home when I was just a second away from ripping off my own clothes seemed like a dangerous idea.

"I'll get them to you. I'll even dry-clean them. And don't worry about the ones you're wearing." I was babbling like an idiot.

"You don't have to do that."

"I don't mind. My dry cleaner knows me at this point. It's no big deal. I'm pretty sure she's been trying to set me up with her son the past three years."

"Anna."

I took a deep breath, and then I got out of his truck. Did I say goodbye? No, apparently Rowan was basically the boogeyman, and I was trying to get into my house before he caught me.

I struggled to find the right key on my fob. It didn't help that my porch light was out, either.

I heard Rowan come up behind me the moment I finally unlocked my front door. But he just followed me inside without another word.

"I'm getting my clothes," he said.

I sighed as I watched him go into the bathroom. The booze I'd drunk at the arcade had already faded away, and I could feel how much my feet hurt in my heels. I slipped them off, then proceeded to take off my bra while padding to my bedroom.

I wanted to sleep. I wanted to be alone. I wanted to peel off these Spanx so I could breathe again.

I finally got into my pajamas, waiting for Rowan to leave. He probably wouldn't even say goodbye. I couldn't blame him, considering I'd been acting like a crazy woman tonight. One second I was all over him, the next, I was telling him nothing could ever happen between us.

I tossed the handful of dresses I'd tried on tonight that I'd left lying on my bed into my closet before collapsing.

"I have to ask," said Rowan from my doorway, "how do you even use these?"

I sat up, then yelped when I saw Rowan holding two different vibrators. I tried to grab them from him, but he just laughed and held them above his head.

"Come on, we're all adults here," he said, his grin lazy.

"You've seriously never seen a sex toy?" I groused.

I poked him in his side, which surprised him enough to let go of the glittery pink vibrator. He still held the royal blue dildo.

"I can't say I've seen a cock this big before," he said,

looking at the dildo more closely. "Who knew a good girl like you liked 'em huge?"

"Christ on a cracker, give it to me before I strangle you." I held the vibrator like a dagger, rather wishing I could use it to impale him.

"Tell me, do you use both of these at the same time? Or do you tease your clit first, getting your pussy wet, then fuck yourself with the dildo?"

His words made my blood heat to boiling. A flush crawled up my chest into my cheeks.

"That's none of your business," I stammered. My tone didn't even sound convincing to me.

"I'm going to take that as a yes." He handed me the dildo. "Show me."

I couldn't breathe. "What?"

"You heard me. Come on, show me. And if you're a good girl, I'll help you."

I shivered. Worse, I was already pulsing wet just from his words alone. He hadn't even touched me.

"Don't tell me you're afraid." Rowan slipped his arm around my waist, pulling me close. I could feel his cock through layers of clothing. "I never took you for a girl who'd back down from a dare."

"Dares are childish."

"I'll help you get started." He pushed my tank top up, slowly brushing against my bare breasts. His other hand delved inside my panties. His index finger explored between my pussy lips, and he smiled in triumph when he found me dripping.

"Show me, Anna." His voice was silky soft. "I want to see you make yourself come."

It was like Rowan had put me into a trance. I couldn't say no. I didn't want to say no. I wanted to let myself do something daring for once in my life.

It didn't help that Rowan was looking at me like he thought I was the sexiest woman alive, wearing old pajamas and my hair in a messy bun. I hadn't even taken off my makeup, and I probably had raccoon eyes.

He slipped off my tank top. He pulled my nipples until I tipped my head back and groaned. I could feel the pinch straight to my clit.

Growling, Rowan kissed me savagely. I dug my fingers into his hair, and then I was flat on my back on the bed with Rowan on top of me. We kissed like we could never get enough of each other. The vibrator and dildo rolled to the edge of the bed. Rowan caught them and handed them to me.

I took off my shorts and panties before Rowan kissed me again. There was something extremely erotic about being naked while he remained fully clothed.

"Show me," he breathed.

I was trembling, but not from fear. It was pure anticipation. It was like electric wires filled my body, and any brush of a hand would set me off. Rowan moved down the bed as I opened my legs to his hungry gaze.

I turned on the vibrator, the buzzing the only noise in the room other than our heavy breathing. I touched the tip to my clit, and I moaned aloud.

Rowan held my leg aloft as I ran the vibrator around the hood of my clit, teasing myself, afraid that it wouldn't take much for me to orgasm.

"God, you're gorgeous," said Rowan, his voice rough. "I

knew your pussy would be pretty. Seeing it all pink and swollen for me. . ."

His words made me dizzy. I struggled to catch my breath. When I nearly dropped the vibrator, I felt Rowan take it from me.

Then he was teasing me with it, seeing how I reacted to every slight movement, every press of the toy against my clit and pussy. I arched, desperate for him to just press it against my clit so I could finally come.

He laughed at me, and his other hand kept me from arching, forcing me to take whatever he wanted to give me.

"Are you close, baby? Because I think you're about to burst," he said as he kissed the inside of my thigh.

"Rowan. . ."

"Say my name again."

"Rowan, Rowan—"

He pressed the vibrator exactly where I wanted it at the same moment he pushed just the tip of the dildo inside me. I screamed, my orgasm hitting me so hard that I was sure that I'd died and gone to heaven. I was racked with shudders, from my head to my toes.

I felt Rowan push the dildo further inside me, stuffing me full, as he circled my throbbing clit. I could feel the edges of another orgasm building.

"Oh my God." I groaned. I didn't care if I woke up the entire neighborhood. "Oh my God!"

"Come on, baby. I want you coming all over this cock. You're so tight—I can't believe you've managed to get this big cock inside before," said Rowan.

He fucked me with the dildo, lightly grazing my clit with the vibrator, until I came a second time. I dug my fingers into my comforter, moaning and writhing, the pleasure nearly unbearable now.

Rowan pulled me into his arms, and I pressed my face against his shoulder. I felt suddenly vulnerable, like I could burst into tears if I weren't careful.

I didn't know how long we lay there together. Rowan eventually lifted his head, moving a few strands of hair from my face.

"I didn't do anything for you," I said. I moved to reach into his pants, but he stopped me.

"It's fine. I need to get going, anyway."

He kissed me and then handed me a blanket. I wrapped it around myself. Being nude in front of him suddenly felt absurd.

Rowan cleared his throat. "I should go," he repeated.

"Okay."

He shot me a look that I couldn't decipher. I followed him to the front door, and after he'd driven away in his truck, I curled up on the living room sofa.

I couldn't find the strength to return to my bedroom, to see the sex toys strewn across the bed, the covers rumpled. I blushed until my cheeks burned.

I'd never, in my entire life, had sex like that before. And it hadn't even been sex-sex. Rowan hadn't gotten off, as far as I could tell. Unless he'd come in his pants and had been too embarrassed to say anything.

The thought of Rowan jizzing his pants was so hilarious that I started giggling like a crazy woman. I danced around my house, feeling like I could take on the world.

But reality crashed into me within moments. Glancing

at my phone, I saw that there were multiple texts from Melanie that I'd missed.

Melanie. Oh God. Hadn't I told Rowan this could never happen? And look what had happened.

Clearly, I wasn't remotely responsible. I was a big fat liar, pants on fire.

I hope the reason you aren't replying is because you're getting your freak on, read the last message from Melanie. It also included several graphic emojis.

I groaned. "What the hell have I done?"

CHAPTER TEN

ANNA

Melanie held up a skimpy red dress in front of me. "How about this one?"

"It looks like lingerie."

"That's the point. You need to branch out."

I took the dress from her, which really was more like a see-through slip with some sequins. I wrinkled my nose. "I don't need to branch out this far."

Melanie sighed but returned the dress to the rack. We'd met up for coffee and shopping at the Beverly Center, and Melanie had insisted on helping me find some new dresses for wedding season.

"You don't have to dress like a grandma when you attend a wedding," Melanie was saying. "Besides, it's LA. Nobody expects you to be modest." She shuddered at the word *modest.*

"Considering I'm wearing a bridesmaid dress more often than not, I don't see why it matters."

Melanie snagged a maxi dress with ruffles and pink flowers. "Come on, how cute is this?"

"It looks like the same pattern of my mom's couch from the nineties."

"Try it on. You never know."

Melanie shoved the dress into my hands. Looking at it more closely, I had to admit, it was cute. If you squinted.

Would Rowan think this dress was cute? The thought was unbidden and caused my cheeks to heat.

It'd been a week since, well, we'd basically had sex. I'd relived that night every day since. I'd dreamed about it more than once, too. Even this morning, I'd awoken with my pussy throbbing and the desperate need to grab my vibrator to finish myself off.

I fanned myself. Melanie shot me a look. "You okay?"

"It's hot in here, don't you think?"

Melanie glanced around. "The AC is on full blast. Besides, it's not crowded."

"I'm probably PMS'ing."

She pressed a hand to my forehead. "You might be coming down with something." She quickly jerked away. "Are you getting sick? Because I cannot get sick. Jaeydyn is coming home Saturday."

Jaeydyn was Melanie's singer hookup. And, yes, his name was really spelled like that. When Melanie had shown me his TikTok page, I'd burst out laughing when I'd seen his name written out. She'd told me I was being mean and wouldn't reply to my texts until the following afternoon.

"I bet Jaeydyn is more likely to infect you with something than I am," I said wryly. "I hope you're using protection with him."

Melanie hit me with her purse. "Don't be vulgar." She sniffed.

"You and I both know that you've gone bareback more than once. I distinctly remember that one guy from that dive bar. Rob? The one who told you that you looked like his mom, and you decided that was super sexy for whatever reason?"

"It was a compliment!"

"Suuuuure."

I picked out a few more dresses and so did Melanie for her to try on. We went to the fitting room, trying on all the dresses and modeling them for each other. When I came out wearing the ruffled floral dress, Melanie's eyes widened.

"I love that! Come on, you look amazing. Look at your boobs!" She even went so far as to give my breasts a bounce.

I had to admit, she'd been right. It did look good on me. It also kept from being too old-fashioned with the open back.

"I hate when you're right," I said.

Melanie beamed. "You should always listen to me."

Melanie decided to buy three different dresses that she definitely did not need. As we were about to check out, Melanie said slyly, "I think the dress you're getting would be great for a first date."

I stopped in my tracks. A woman behind us nearly collided into me, and she shot me an annoyed look as she huffed away.

"Melanie Jean, what does that mean? And what have you done?"

Melanie held up her hands. "Nothing! I mean, nothing that's a huge deal."

"I don't believe you. Spill."

My best friend wouldn't look me in the eye now. "I might've told my coworker that you're single."

"Which coworker?"

"Um, Preston?"

I groaned. "No, not the guy with seven kids. The one who was in a cult? Melanie, come on."

"He's really nice! He's cute, too. And he told me he doesn't want any more kids."

"Shocking. I thought he wanted an entire baseball team?"

"He's not in the cult anymore! I swear. He's just a regular guy." Melanie gave me her best puppy-eyed stare. "He even wears jeans now. Apparently that was definitely not allowed in the cult so it was a big deal for him."

"So you told him I was single, or was there something else?"

Melanie started walking. "I'm hungry. Are you? Because I really want some poke."

"Melanie!"

When I grabbed her arm, she blurted, "I might've told him you'd go on a date with him."

I gaped at her. "You did not."

"Ma'am, is this woman bothering you?" asked one of the sales associates.

I let go of Melanie's arm, but not before Melanie replied, "Yes, she's being a big jerkface. You can tell her I said those exact words."

"We're friends," I said. "Mel, tell him we're friends."

Melanie sniffed and walked away.

The sales associate looked nonplussed. He also began

reaching for his walkie-talkie. I really didn't want to spend time with mall security because Melanie was in a snit.

I found Melanie at a checkout station on the other side of the store. She didn't acknowledge me, but she waited for me to pay for my dresses, so that was a start.

"Why are you mad at me?" I asked her.

"Because you always do this. I try to do nice things for you, but you just complain and make it seem like I'm the one in the wrong."

"I didn't ask you to set me up on a blind date."

"No, but I know you're lonely." When I opened my mouth to refute her, she held up a hand. "I'm your friend. I know you, probably even better than you know yourself. You haven't dated anybody since Darren, and that was three years ago."

"Being single isn't a death sentence."

"I also know that you'd like a relationship. But you don't put in any effort to find someone. Tell me I'm wrong."

I gaped at her. Melanie wasn't usually this assertive. I also hated that, just like with the dress, she was right. I'd avoided dating and relationships after Darren because I hadn't wanted to try. I'd thrown myself into my work and then wondered why I was still alone at night.

"That doesn't mean I want to date your coworker," I pointed out.

"Maybe. It's just a date. Not a marriage. Get a drink with him, see how it goes. You might like him."

I hated that she'd boxed me into a corner. Refusing the date would make it seem like I was refusing Melanie's attempts at doing something nice for me.

I thought of Rowan. "What if I'm already interested in another guy?" I said suddenly.

Melanie narrowed her eyes at me. "Who? You haven't mentioned anybody lately."

"I'm speaking hypothetically."

"Are you dating somebody else, then?"

I was tempted to lie. But then I'd have to explain who this mystery guy was. And it wasn't like I could tell her it was her ex-boyfriend of all people.

I shot her a tight smile. "No, there's nobody else."

I SPENT that evening at home—alone. I was on my second glass of wine when I decided to look up Rowan online. I'd applauded myself for not going sleuthing before this evening. But apparently tonight my self-control lost the battle against morbid curiosity.

To my annoyance, I didn't find much. He wasn't on Instagram. He had an old LinkedIn profile that hadn't been updated since he'd left AppVille. No Twitter account, either. When I found his Facebook profile, I was surprised he even had an account.

His Facebook profile had a few posts from three, four, five years ago posted by Rowan himself. I tried to find any evidence that he'd dated Melanie, but there was nothing. Just photos of hikes he'd taken and beer festivals he'd attended. If he'd ever posted about his relationship with Melanie, he'd scrubbed it.

Near the top, though, were new pictures. They were tagged photos. I clicked on the tagger. Her name was Alexis, and she had the perfect LA glow, along with the perfectly sculpted body. Her dark brown hair went to her waist; she had the perfect pout and nose.

"So much plastic surgery," I muttered.

When I looked at the photos Alexis had tagged of Rowan, I felt sick. In one picture, Alexis was sitting on Rowan's lap. He was grinning at the camera. In another that was clearly a selfie, Alexis was kissing Rowan on the cheek. They looked like they were with a bunch of other people at a bar.

I tossed my phone aside. I didn't need to see anything else. Besides, it wasn't like Rowan and I were dating or exclusive. We'd messed around once. I shouldn't feel I was going to throw up.

But that green-eyed snake of jealousy circled around my heart and squeezed—hard. I couldn't compete with a woman like Alexis. I was short; my nose had a decided bump; my lips were average-sized. I didn't get spray tans because I didn't want to spend the money. My breasts were on the small side. Compared to Alexis, I couldn't measure up.

I felt stupidly near tears. I hated myself for it. I got up and got myself another glass of wine.

"He can go out with anyone he wants," I told myself as I tried to find something to watch, to take my mind off of Rowan. "He can sleep with Alexis if he wants. He's not my boyfriend. He never was. I'm being an idiot."

I couldn't even watch a rom-com like I usually would to feel better. I ended up turning off the TV and staring up at the ceiling as I stewed in my own misery.

My phone beeped. *Can I give you Preston's number?* Melanie had messaged.

I thought of Rowan's stupid, happy grin in that photo with Alexis on his lap. Had he even waited twenty-four hours from when he'd made me come before getting in bed with another woman?

Yeah, that's fine, I replied. *What's Preston's number? I'll put it in my phone.*

Awesome! I bet you two will hit it off. I swear he's a normal guy. I mean, minus all the kids. Maybe ignore that part.

Kinda hard to ignore that, but okay. He just better not bring them along.

Melanie just replied with a laughing emoji. Then she sent me Preston's number.

I opened a message to send to Preston. I felt a buzz throughout my entire body as I began typing.

When I sent Preston that first text message, Rowan didn't come into my thoughts again that night.

CHAPTER ELEVEN

ROWAN

Emily pointed to a bunch of eucalyptus trees on the outskirts of my property. "Are those dead?"

I squinted. To be honest, most of the greenery around here—besides the orange trees—looked pretty dead. But this was southern California. We lived in a fucking desert. After last week's rainstorm, though, the trees looked as though they had a little bit of life left in them.

"Because if they're dead," Emily was saying, "do you think they could be cut down?"

Alejo shot me a look that said, *Sorry, bro.*

"I don't think we'll want to deal with cutting down trees," Anna replied, her smile steady on her face. "Besides, you'll want as much shade as you can get. Even in the late afternoon."

Emily and Alejo went to look at the trees in question, leaving me with Anna. It was a struggle to stand next to her and act like nothing had happened between us. Every time I heard her voice, I thought of the way she'd moaned and screamed my name that night at her place.

I should regret that I'd lost my self-control. But I didn't. I felt triumphant. It didn't help that Anna's cheeks had been pink the entire time she'd been here.

"I promise I won't let Emily destroy your property," said Anna.

"I'd appreciate that."

"But if the trees are dead—"

I raised an eyebrow. "What, you'll stop by one afternoon to cut them down?"

"Of course not. I'd just suggest you pay somebody to do that for you."

I guffawed. I'd had to restrain a few guffaws this morning during this meeting. Emily apparently had grand plans about turning this space into her vision of a perfect wedding.

She'd chattered about fairy lights, and pampas grass, and asked if I had a hexagon arch. The fuck was a hexagon arch? Weren't arches supposed to be *arch*-shaped?

"Is there a way to install some fans in the barn?" Anna's question broke through my thoughts. "Or better yet, air-conditioning?"

"You want to pay to install ductwork? Be my guest."

Anna wrinkled her nose. "Fair point. Hopefully it won't be too hot. If not, then we'll just have to supply everyone with plenty of cold beer."

I smiled slyly. "Alcohol sure helps loosen people up, doesn't it?"

Anna just clutched her clipboard and raised her chin. "Emily wants us. Come on."

We spent the rest of the morning figuring out various logistics for the wedding. It ended up being a whole list of tasks that made my head hurt. When Anna handed me the list, I could just see my entire bank account being drained.

"This investment better fucking pay off," I grumbled, "otherwise you'll be the one paying me back, Dyer."

Anna just patted my arm. "Don't get your panties in a twist. This place is going to be so popular you'll have to beat people away with a stick."

"I've already told some friends of mine about this place," said Emily. Her eyes were sparkling. "One of my sisters is waiting for your website to go live. I think she checks every day to see if it's up."

I grimaced. "Great."

Alejo laughed and slapped me on the shoulder. "Don't look too excited."

"Yeah, don't look too excited that you have a business opportunity that could make you tons of money," Anna said, sarcasm dripping from her voice.

I felt a little guilty then. This was a great opportunity. I wouldn't be doing it if I thought it wasn't. But at the same time, a part of me wanted everyone to get the hell off my property and leave me alone.

How did I turn into an irascible old man already at the age of thirty-three?

Anna was explaining something to Emily. My ears pricked up when I heard her say, "I can't meet this Saturday night, sorry. Sunday would be better." Her cheeks turned red.

Emily looked like the cat that caught the canary. "Anna Dyer, spill! You have a secret. Are you going on a date?"

I felt my chest tighten. "Yeah, Anna," I drawled, "are you going on a date?"

Alejo shot me a strange look, but I ignored it.

Anna was writing something on her clipboard. "It's not a big deal. My friend Melanie set something up—"

"So it is a date! Who is it? Maybe we know him!" said Emily.

"Probably not. It's a blind date. It's one of Melanie's coworkers."

"What's his name?" I asked.

Anna narrowed her eyes at me. "Preston."

"Sounds like a douche."

"You don't even know him!"

I shrugged. "I know a douchey name when I hear one."

Emily and Alejo's gazes were darting back and forth between us.

"I'm sure he'll be a nice guy," Emily said while Alejo remarked, "It *is* a frat guy name."

"It's none of your business, anyway," said Anna. Then she plastered a fake smile on her face. "Anyway, let's schedule for Sunday. I'll be free all day."

"Maybe not in the early morning," I muttered.

Anna elbowed me the second Emily and Alejo turned to look at a hawk circling overhead.

"Can you *not?"* she hissed.

I just shot her an obnoxious smile.

Before the engaged couple left, Alejo came up to me while Emily and Anna puttered around in the barn one last time.

"What was that all about?" Alejo asked.

"What was what?"

"Oh, come on. Whatever that was with Anna. You guys look like you're one second away from tearing each other's clothes off. Or ripping each other's eyes out. It's hard to tell."

I scowled. "You're imagining things."

"Dude, if you like her, just ask her out. Pretty sure that's a thing people still do."

"I don't like her. She's prissy and annoying. She always thinks she's right."

Alejo just chuckled. "Okay, then. If you guys want to keep eye-fucking each other, go for it. Just don't let it mess up our wedding. Because then I'll have to kill you, if Emily doesn't get to you first."

"You heard Anna. She has a blind date."

"So? She's not married."

I didn't know how to explain this strange, thorny feeling that made me want to strangle somebody. I preferred to remain calm and collected in most things. But something about Anna riled me up.

You're jealous. Come on, admit it. You're jealous she's going out with some other guy after you fucked her senseless.

Anna could date whoever she wanted. She wasn't mine to get jealous over.

"Even if I wanted to date her," I said quietly, "she's made it clear it won't happen. Because I dated her best friend."

"What? When was that?"

"Five years ago."

Alejo's eyes widened. "Seriously? I thought you were going to tell me it was five *months* ago. That's fucking crazy. Is her friend still in love with you or something?"

I shrugged. "I doubt it. We didn't end on great terms.

But apparently she got Anna to promise not to have anything to do with me."

"Women are terrifying." Right as Alejo said those words, Emily came bounding up to him, saying something about renting some farm animals for the wedding.

"It'll be a petting zoo! And we can get pictures with them! Come on, how cool would that be?" said Emily.

Alejo sighed. "We'll talk about it later."

AFTER ANNA and I waved the happy couple goodbye, Anna looked at me like she wanted to murder me. If she weren't half a head shorter than me, I would've been intimidated.

"What is your fucking problem?" she fumed.

I just cocked my head to the side, which seemed only to annoy Anna further.

"You know what? This whole thing is so childish—"

She went inside my house to get her bag. I followed her, mostly because I didn't trust her not to start breaking things. Besides, Anna in a temper was always a sight to behold, and I didn't want to miss a minute of it.

"You seem mad," I said, barely restraining a smile.

"No, really? What tipped you off?" Anna grabbed her bag and tried to stomp out of the house.

I caught her by the elbow. "Come on, you can't leave like this."

"I don't understand you." Anna shook her head. "One second, you're cold, the next, you're all over me. The next, you're mad that I'm going on a blind date when you've already been with another woman since last week!"

I stared at her. "The fuck are you talking about?"

"Oh my God. I am not doing this. This is so high school—"

"Explain." I gritted my teeth. "Please."

Anna looked incredulous. "Seriously?" She pulled out her phone and then showed me the screen. "Look, you can bang whoever you want, but don't act like the dog in the manger if I want to get some, too."

The photos were of me and a friend of a friend, photos I'd never seen before. Then I laughed when I realized.

"Those pictures are from three years ago," I said.

Anna scoffed. "What about the caption? Come on, I'm not that stupid."

"Look at my hair. It's shorter in these pictures than it is now."

Anna scrutinized the pictures, narrowing her eyes and then zooming in to see more closely. Then she let out a huff.

"Okay. I guess your hair is shorter there. Barely, but I see it." She shot me an annoyed look. "But I still don't get why you got all mad about me going on a blind date. Just because we messed around doesn't mean you get to be all growly and possessive."

I smiled as I maneuvered Anna in between my body and the wall, neatly trapping her. She realized it too late. Crossing her arms, she refused to look at me.

"I don't know why you make me all 'growly and possessive,'" I admitted. "But the thought of you with another man makes me want to rip out his throat."

I watched in amusement as a tide of red flooded her cheeks. "That's stupid." Her voice was squeaky.

"Maybe. Or maybe there's something about you that's

just irresistible. . ." I touched a lock of hair that had fallen across her face. "I haven't stopped thinking about that night, you know."

She swallowed. "Me either."

"Then why agree to go on a date with Frat Boy Douchecanoe?"

Her lips twitched. "He's not a frat boy! If you must know, he just got out of a cult. He has seven kids, even."

I stared at her. "You can't be serious."

"Totally."

"You want to be a stepmother to seven kids?"

"No! I mean, whoever said we were getting married? Geez, you're worse than Melanie."

At those words, we both froze. Anna quickly ducked under my arm before I could react.

"Anna. . ."

She flinched. "We can't keep doing this." Even as she said the words, I could feel how she didn't mean them. Not really.

I took her bag; she didn't resist me. After setting it down on the counter, I turned her so she was facing me.

"Whoever said we were getting married?" I quoted. At her surprised blink, I added, "Can't we have fun without letting things get serious? And it's not like Melanie ever has to know."

I touched Anna's bottom lip. My cock hardened when she licked the tip of my thumb.

"I'm not good at keeping secrets," she admitted.

"Then you'll just have to try very, very hard this time."

I began pulling bobby pins from her hair until it tumbled down her shoulders. She so rarely wore it down that seeing her with her hair down for once was unbearably erotic.

"Rowan," she sighed.

"Yes?" I kissed her throat.

"What are we doing?"

"Oh, baby, if you have to ask, I'm doing a shit job."

I then lifted her into my arms; she squealed in surprise. I carried her to the back of the house and tossed her onto my bed. She shot me an annoyed look.

"Can you not toss me around like a sack of flour?" she groused.

"But you're so small and portable." I climbed onto the bed and pinned her down. "And it's fun."

"It's not fun for me!"

I reached under her skirt and groaned when I discovered she was wearing a thong.

"Anna," I said, my voice hoarse now. "Shut the hell up and enjoy the ride."

To my surprise, she fluttered her lashes as she smiled seductively. The look went straight to my cock, and I could barely restrain a groan.

"But you never explained what we're going to do," she complained. She stuck out her bottom lip. "I'm so confused. You need to teach me, Professor."

I'd never considered myself particularly kinky in bed. I liked a good, straightforward fuck. No whips or chains or awkward roleplay.

But Anna staring up at me with feigned apprehension and calling me Professor?

Shit, I was *fucked.*

"Baby, I'm going to plow you until you beg me to stop."

I yanked her skirt off and tossed it away. "You'll be so stuffed with my cock that you'll beg for mercy. And I'll feel you come all over my cock over and over again, just like I felt when I fucked you last week."

Her eyes were shining. "Sounds good to me," she whispered before wrapping her arms around me and pulling me down for a kiss.

CHAPTER TWELVE

ANNA

We were doing this. We were really, truly, doing this. It felt like a dream as Rowan kissed me, his hands roving down my body like he was searching for the holy grail. Every nerve in my body came alight. When he squeezed my ass, massaging both cheeks, I wanted to climb his body like a tree.

"Patience," he intoned. He smiled down at me. "Otherwise this is going to be over before it's begun."

"Sounds like you're the one who's going to jizz in his pants." I began unzipping his jeans, reaching inside his boxers to stroke his half-hard cock. "Do you want me to help you?"

Rowan let me squeeze and stroke him for a few long moments until he pushed my hand away. "Naked. Now."

We stripped out of our clothes at record speed. For a brief second, I felt embarrassed, being nude in the middle of the day. Every time I'd had sex, it had been with the lights off.

But the heated look on Rowan's face made me realize I

was being silly. He looked at me like he couldn't wait to devour me. It was both terrifying and exhilarating at the same time.

"God, you're fucking beautiful." Rowan tossed pillows aside, growling when he couldn't get the comforter pushed down to reveal the sheets beneath.

"Somebody is desperate," I remarked.

Rowan tangled his hands in my hair, tilting my head back as he kissed me deeply. "Oh, now that's a challenge."

I thought of how he'd tormented me that night at my place. The thought of him playing my body like a fiddle a second time? I nearly came right then and there.

Rowan plunged his tongue into my mouth as he massaged my breasts, pinching my nipples until they were bright red and sensitive. When he sucked one into his mouth, I moaned, the sensation going straight to my clit.

"I want to eat this pussy," Rowan said. He pushed my legs apart, and he groaned when he saw how wet I was already.

"Damn, baby, you're already soaked." His eyes were dark as his gaze collided with mine. "I think somebody wants to be fucked."

Rowan plunged his tongue into my mouth as he massaged my breasts, pinching my nipples until they were bright red and sensitive. When he sucked one into his mouth, I moaned, the sensation going straight to my clit.

"I want to eat this pussy," Rowan said. He pushed my legs apart, and he groaned when he saw how wet I was already.

"Damn, baby, you're already soaked." His eyes were

dark as his gaze collided with mine. "I think somebody wants to be fucked."

"So poetic."

He yanked my body forward and lay down on his stomach, taking a moment to situate himself.

"Ya good? Ready yet?" I asked with a laugh.

He gave me a wry look. "I like to be comfortable when I feast."

And feast he did. I knew Rowan wasn't a man to do anything by halves. He buried his face in my pussy, making me gasp, although there was hardly any reason to be surprised. Or maybe I was just surprised at how thoroughly he went about the job.

Sure, I'd had a few good oral sessions here and there. But this? This was nothing like I'd ever experienced.

Rowan parted me with gentle fingers, stroking down one side and then the other. I shivered when he licked inside my pussy, spreading my juices across my vulva, his tongue just barely touching my throbbing clit.

"I've wanted to do this since that night at Trevor's wedding," he said in between licks. "I wanted to yank your panties down and fuck your sweet pussy with my tongue until you came all over my face."

I shuddered. "I probably would've let you," I admitted.

That made him laugh, but it was an evil laugh. When he started licking around the perimeter of my clit, I grabbed at his hair.

"Didn't I already tell you to be patient?" he said.

I just gripped his hair harder. Unfortunately for me, that just seemed to egg him on.

He tilted my pelvis higher. The sounds of him eating my

pussy, along with our commingled groans, were almost unbearable. I could feel my wetness drip down my ass crack. I'd never been this wet in my life.

Rowan captured my clit with his lips and sucked. He sucked so hard that I arched off the table in shock. When he combined the suction with his fingers, the air whooshed from my lungs.

"Come for me, baby," Rowan was saying, moving his fingers faster inside my tightening pussy. "Come on my face."

I flushed bright red, but I was beyond embarrassment now. I moved with his fingers, the orgasm at my fingertips, when I felt one of his fingers circle my asshole. When he just breached that tight ring, my orgasm hit me like a ton of bricks.

"Fuck!" I screamed, my entire body bending in half. "Oh my God—"

Rowan kissed my pussy one last time before standing up. His erection was nearly parallel to his body, long and red and hard. Rowan wiped his chin, his expression dark and purposeful. Then he kissed me.

His cock rubbed against my still sensitive pussy. I arched, desperate for him to fill me, but he just kept rubbing it through my dripping pussy lips.

"You want me?" he rasped. His fingers were wet as he stroked my cheek.

I grabbed his cock and squeezed. "If you don't fuck me soon, I'm going to lose my goddamn mind."

He chuckled. Then he placed my legs over his arms, opening me wide, the head of his cock pushing at the entrance to my pussy.

I watched, entranced, as Rowan slowly pushed inside me until he filled me to the hilt. I started shivering. It was almost too much sensation. The tips of my fingers down to the tips of my toes tingled.

"You're so fucking tight," he said with a groan as he slowly pulled out and then sank back inside me. I watched his cock grow wetter with every stroke, while I wondered if he was getting bigger with every thrust.

"Look at how perfect we fit." He was breathing hard now, his cheeks flushed. "It's like your pussy was made for me."

I just whimpered. I dug my nails into his shoulders as he fucked me harder. The sounds, the smells, the sensations, all of them coalesced until I could feel a second orgasm building inside me.

"Rowan," I gasped. "Oh my God—"

"Come on my cock. I want to feel it." He kissed me hard, nipping at my bottom lip as he pinched one of my nipples. When he slammed into me again and again, making the bed squeak and groan, I turned into a begging, pathetic mess of a woman.

My release hit me, the pleasure nearly painful. I yelled Rowan's name just a moment before he came with a long, low groan. I felt him fill up my pussy with his cum, and it lengthened my orgasm until it felt like it would never end.

"Fuck," Rowan was saying in my ear. He kissed me and then lifted me from the table. "Fuck, fuck, fuck."

When we collapsed onto the bed together, his cock still inside me, I had a feeling I'd never want to leave this bed again.

I AWOKE to an empty bed and a rumbling stomach. I winced when I realized that I was sore; then I promptly blushed when the memories from earlier burst inside my brain.

I pulled the comforter up over my head. But that only made things worse, because it smelled like Rowan. Sighing, I sat up, taking in my surroundings.

I'd never been inside Rowan's house beyond using the bathroom once or twice. I'd assumed it had been like any other bachelor pad, which meant minimal furniture except for maybe a couch, a large TV, and a mattress on the floor. Bonus points if he used cardboard boxes for tables.

I was pleased to see that not only did Rowan have a bed frame, but he also had an actual nightstand. And he had a lamp. And a bookshelf. But I realized quickly that his bookshelf didn't have many books. The titles I could read seemed entirely related to farming and growing produce.

Seeing some clothes on the floor nearby was the only real indication that a real human lived here. There was one picture on the wall of—you guessed it—a grove of orange trees. At least it was framed, I reasoned.

Being the snoop that I was, I couldn't help but open his nightstand drawer. But all it contained were his phone charger, some ear plugs, and a few expired condoms.

Condoms. I felt the blood drain from my face. Motherfucking hell, we didn't use a condom. We'd been so insane for each other that we hadn't stopped to think rationally.

"What're you doing?" Rowan asked.

I slammed the nightstand drawer shut. "Looking for some gum," I lied. "You have any?"

"No, sorry." He was wearing his boxers and holding two mugs. He handed me one and then pulled a roll of cookies from the waistband. "I figured you'd be hungry."

I immediately ripped open the packet. "Thanks," I said through a mouthful of cookie.

"I could make us something. It's near dinnertime." He glanced at his watch. "But there's not much here. I need to go on a grocery run."

I wondered if he was trying to find a reason to get me to leave. I drank my tea, my gut clenching.

"Well, this is awkward," I said finally.

Rowan snorted, then looked away. "I feel like I should apologize," he began.

I felt my body grow cold. "Why?"

"Because. I acted like an animal this afternoon." He rubbed the back of his neck. "And now you won't look at me."

"That's because you won't look at me!"

That made him chuckle. "So, you're okay?"

I shrugged. "We had sex. Although let's be honest, we kinda already had sex. Now we've had sex-sex. Penis in vagina sex. The real deal. The stuff of legends—"

He pinched my lips closed. "Please, no more."

I batted his hand away. "Speaking of having your penis in my vagina. . ." *Wow, great segue, Anna.* "We didn't use a condom."

Rowan stared at me. Then he swore, getting up from the bed and nearly spilling his own mug of tea. "I could've sworn—" he muttered. "Why didn't you say something?"

My jaw dropped. "Uh, okay, we both fucked up, but seriously?"

"And you're sure?"

"I mean, based on, um, the evidence now on your sheets, no rubber barrier was involved."

Rowan looked grim. "Are you on birth control?"

"No." When he swore again, I sighed. "I'll get the morning-after pill before I go home. It'll be fine. I should start my period soon."

"You'll tell me? When you start it?"

I gaped at him. "Um, I guess?" As I watched him pace back and forth, my annoyance grew. "I mean, will a text do, or do you want photographic evidence?"

He glared at me. "If you get pregnant—"

"Then we'll deal with it. We aren't sixteen, Rowan. Also, I'm clean. Are you? That's what I'm concerned about."

Now he looked offended. "Of course I am."

Men. "Great!" I said, too chipper now. "Then no chlamydia for us. But if a fetus starts growing inside me, I'll give you a ring."

He didn't look amused. He looked like he wanted to throw himself out the nearest window. "You're surprisingly blasé about all of this."

"And you're being a jackass. Because it sounds like you're insinuating that I'm trying to baby trap you, which is just gross. We got caught up in the moment. I'm not proud of it, but if there are consequences, we'll deal with them. I promise you, I have zero interest in our DNA creating some monster baby."

Rowan took a deep breath. Then another. "Sorry," he said shortly. "I didn't mean to insinuate that. I know you wouldn't do that."

"Thank you."

He set his mug on top of his dresser. "It's getting late."

I knew my cue to leave. When I got up to dress, Rowan left and quickly returned with my clothes.

As I dressed, I felt stupidly close to tears. Normally, I would be the one freaking out about the whole no-condom thing. And I was, but not for the reasons Rowan was.

I was panicking because I'd lost all control back there. Logic had fallen to the wayside. It was like Rowan had put a spell on me and I'd been powerless to resist.

You can't blame him, I told myself. I wanted to, but that wouldn't be fair. I wanted him. And I still did.

I thought of Melanie and felt sick. I'd betrayed her multiple times now. I could've written off the first hookup as a one-off. But this round? Now it was a pattern.

Rowan walked me to my car. "Let me know," he said, his hands in his pockets.

"We'll be seeing each other soon. We're still doing the plus-one thing, right?"

He nodded. Then, surprising me, he gently tilted my face up and kissed me. It was such a sweet, tender brushing of lips that it made me want to burst into tears.

"Until next time," he murmured, making me wonder what, exactly, next time would entail.

CHAPTER THIRTEEN

ANNA

I sat down on the emerald green velvet settee, lounging like an old Hollywood starlet. "How about this one?"

"I feel like I should be feeding you grapes right now," Rowan replied.

I had to admit, the thought of Rowan doing just that sent a shiver down my spine. Or maybe it was because he was standing over me, looking all muscular and handsome and stupidly attractive. My heart started pounding. It was ridiculous, how easily affected I was by this man. He wasn't even touching me.

I sat up, so quickly that I had to wait a moment for the blood to return to my brain.

"Do they really need furniture for a wedding?" asked Rowan. He was poking at the arm of a leather sofa. "I thought tables and chairs were all that you needed for a wedding."

"Rowan, darling, we're creating *ambiance.* Also, people like to sit on couches and fluffy chairs. It's fun. It also helps people feel more comfortable socializing." I shot Rowan a wry grin. "Maybe you should try it."

"Ha ha," he said, rolling his eyes.

When I'd initially told Emily and Alejo that I'd help them in choosing rentals for their wedding, I'd expected to do that alone. Yet here I was, shopping for furniture and other accoutrements with Rowan like that was totally normal.

You fucked each other silly and this is why you think it's weird? I reminded myself.

I had to repress the lurid memories that rose to the surface. Although I should've felt guilty, I couldn't. The only thing I could feel was that I wanted to slip back into Rowan's bed for another round. And then maybe never leave.

"Can I help you two find something?" a sales assistant asked Rowan, her white teeth blinding as she smiled.

"We're looking for wedding stuff," was Rowan's unhelpful reply.

The sales assistant's eyes lit up. "Oh, congratulations! When is the big day?"

Before Rowan could correct her, I took his arm and squeezed it. "Not for another year, but you know weddings. Can't do anything last minute."

I could feel Rowan glaring at the top of my head. I was glad he couldn't shoot lasers from his eyes, because he would've scorched me.

"We rent out to tons of weddings. Where is the wedding going to be? And what time? I can offer some suggestions," the sales assistant said.

I let her show me around, even though I'd been to this

store many times before. Rowan followed at a distance, saying very little.

Why had I let this woman think we were engaged?

"Now, have you thought about centerpieces?" the sales assistant asked.

Rowan picked up a tall vase, frowning. "This is huge."

"Oh, those vases are great for super tall centerpieces. You can fit up to a hundred roses in that one, believe it or not."

Rowan blinked. "In one vase?"

"I'll admit, I'm not a big fan of the huge centerpieces. Makes it hard to see people around the table," I said.

The sales assistant fluttered her hands. "Oh, sure, sure. Have you looked at bud vases? We're seeing a lot of couples preferring them over the traditional large vases."

I could feel Rowan growing bored. He wandered away, letting me negotiate with Shannon, our chipper sales assistant. When I'd finally taken photos of everything that I could send over to Emily and Alejo, I couldn't find Rowan anywhere.

I wandered outside. The sun was bright and made my eyes hurt, especially since the warehouse had been dim by comparison. I followed the sound of male voices.

"You'll want to irrigate when the soil is dry but not bone-dry," Rowan was saying. "I've found that works the best while using the least amount of water."

"Tried that, didn't work," the other man replied, shaking his head. "I ended up with only a quarter of my usual crop. But I was afraid of using too much water, what with the drought and all."

"Are your trees young or mature? That also makes a difference."

I listened, rather enthralled despite the subject matter. Rowan was animated, his eyes lit up and his expression enthused. I'd never seen him look like that when we'd discussed Emily and Alejo's wedding. I had to admit, it suited him.

"Honey, are you ready to go?" I asked.

Rowan shot me a wry glance. "Baby, I'm always ready," he replied, his voice rough.

"You two come from the warehouse?" the man asked.

"We're shopping for wedding rentals." I took Rowan's hand and squeezed it.

"Wedding rentals, huh?" The man shook his head. "My missus and I got married in the basement of our church. Probably didn't spend more than a few hundred bucks. What the hell do you need to rent? Besides your tux." He chuckled.

"Weddings are a little more expensive nowadays," I said.

"Expensive? It's ridiculous! You gonna spend tens of thousands on one day? Better save that money for the divorce." The man laughed at his own joke.

I was starting to get annoyed. If I had a dollar for how many times someone had said something just like that, I'd be a millionaire.

I opened my mouth to reply, but Rowan said, "Whatever makes the bride happy."

I gazed out the window as Rowan drove me home, saying very little.

"You're annoyed," he said, startling me.

"What? No, I'm not."

"Don't let what that guy said get under your skin."

"It's not—" I sighed. I sighed again when Rowan's truck rolled to a stop, traffic now crawling along the 210. "It's just frustrating feeling like I have to justify my work all the time."

"Who says you have to?"

I snorted. "Has anyone ever insinuated that your job is frivolous? Or downright stupid?"

"You'd be surprised."

"Seriously?"

Rowan shrugged. "When I quit my tech job, there were plenty of people who thought I was crazy to start growing oranges instead."

"But nobody tells you that growing oranges is stupid, either."

He frowned. "What's your point?"

"My point is," I said slowly, "that with weddings, you can't win no matter what you do. If you elope to save money, then you're being cruel in excluding your friends and family. If you spend money on a wedding, then you're being extravagant and wasteful. But if you don't have a wedding, then are you really married? It's all a catch-22."

I blew out a breath. "Look, I realize that I'm not out here curing cancer. But I love my job, and I want my clients to have amazing weddings, no matter what they cost. Even if they gave me a budget of five hundred dollars, I'd make it work."

"If you could pull off a wedding that cheap in Los Angeles," said Rowan with a smile, "even I'd be impressed."

I laughed. "Wow, was that compliment?"

"Don't get used to it, Dyer."

I rolled my eyes. Traffic started moving again, albeit at half the speed limit. I rolled down my window and let my arm hang, feeling the light desert breeze against my fingers.

"Why did you act like we were engaged?" asked Rowan.

I froze. In my annoyance, I'd nearly forgotten about that little farce. I shrugged, trying to sound casual now.

"I thought it'd be funny. Mostly to rile you," I admitted.

Rowan didn't look convinced. "Really."

"Yeah, really."

"Hmm."

Hmm? Seriously? That was all he had to say about it?

Anna, stop acting like there's something real between you. Besides the insane chemistry.

"I'm sorry," I said finally, blushing. "I shouldn't have done that. I'm sure it made you uncomfortable."

Rowan's hands tightened on the steering wheel. "It didn't."

My heart squeezed. "What?"

"I wasn't uncomfortable." When his gaze collided with mine, my entire body warmed. "I was just surprised, that's all."

I licked my lips. My throat was dry. It felt like I couldn't draw enough air into my lungs.

"Do you even want to get married someday?" I asked. I could've bitten my tongue in half right after I said the words. *Way to keep things casual.*

Rowan seemed unfazed. "I shouldn't tell you this."

Now I was intrigued. "But you are anyway. . .?"

"Because you'll tease me for it." His lips quirked. "But when I was younger, I always assumed I'd be married with a kid or two by the time I was thirty. But obviously, that didn't happen."

I didn't laugh. "I think that's a pretty normal goal."

"That's just it: it was a goal because that's what society expects. You find a girl, you marry her, you have babies. You get a good job to support your family. She stays home with the kids. Etcetera."

"Rowan, I don't know if you're aware, but women work *outside* the home nowadays," I joked.

"You know what I mean," was his rough reply. He began tapping his fingers on the steering wheel. "Why the fuck haven't we moved in the last five minutes?"

"Because it's LA. So are you telling me that since you're over the age of thirty that you don't want to get married anymore?"

"No." He rubbed the back of his neck. "I don't know. I think I've just gotten to a point in my life where I don't expect it to happen anymore."

Oh God, my heart ached at that admission. I could hear the loneliness in Rowan's voice, the expectation that he wouldn't have anyone to share his life with.

I hated it. It made me understand him better. It made me want to say something ridiculous, like *I can be that woman for you.* I had the sudden image of him coming home as I was cooking dinner, a baby in the highchair, Rowan coming up behind me to kiss the back of my neck.

"Well, you're hardly an old maid," I joked. "You're not even forty. You have plenty of time."

Rowan glanced at me. "What about you? Isn't your biological clock ticking or whatever?"

"Um, gross. Also, no. I'm only thirty. I have plenty of

time. And who knows if I'll even want kids? I'm not worried about it. And I guess if I was really desperate for kids, I could marry Preston. He has seven of 'em already."

I was lying. I was worried about it. Oh, not the kid thing, but sometimes at night, I wondered if I'd always be single. It was easy enough to find a guy for the night. Finding a guy you wanted to spend the rest of your life with? It felt like an impossible task.

Which was ironic, considering that my job was literally all about celebrating people finding their other halves.

When Rowan finally dropped me off, I hesitated to get out. Did I not want this little sojourn of ours to end?

Now you're just acting desperate.

"We have a wedding on Saturday," I reminded Rowan. When he said nothing, I asked, "You okay with us still being each other's plus-ones?"

"We made a bargain, didn't we?"

He sounded irritated now.

"Um, yeah. I guess." I could feel the tension rising inside the truck.

"Did you go out with him?" Rowan demanded. "That frat boy. Preston."

I widened my eyes in astonishment. And I realized, as I stared at Rowan, that he was jealous.

Jealous. I couldn't believe it. I had to clap a hand over my mouth to keep from giggling like a teenage girl.

"You mean, did I go on a blind date only a day after we had sex?" I asked.

Rowan scowled. "Answer the question."

"Oh my God. No, I canceled. Is that what you wanted to hear? I canceled, because it felt weird to go out with another man when I'd just slept with another. I know people do it all the time, but—"

Rowan's hand cupped the back of my head, and he pulled me forward, kissing me roughly. I made a sound of surprise, which turned into a moan when he slipped his tongue inside my mouth.

The kiss ended far too soon. We were both breathing hard; I half-expected the truck windows to be steamy à la the carriage in *Titanic.*

"I want to see you again," said Rowan.

"Isn't that what you're doing right now?"

He smiled. "I want to fuck you again. Does that clarify things?"

I struggled to breathe. "Samesies," was my stupid reply.

"Saturday then." He kissed me one last time and then like the gentleman he was, he told me to get my sexy little ass out of his truck.

CHAPTER FOURTEEN

ROWAN

My mom called me at the crack of dawn on Sunday morning. I let it go to voicemail, only to hear my phone ring a second time. I groaned and grabbed the offending electronic.

"Who died?" I answered. I yawned loudly.

Mom just laughed. "Nobody! Why would you say such a thing? I just haven't talked to you in forever."

I squinted at the clock on my nightstand. "It's six in the morning."

"And don't you have work to do?"

"Which would preclude me from talking to you on the phone."

Mom clucked her tongue. "You know I told you that you had to become a morning person if you wanted to run a farm. You can't farm in the middle of the night. Harold!"

I winced. My mom called my dad's name a second time, and then suddenly I was talking to both of them.

"Harold, it's Rowan. Yes, he's awake. I'll ask him. Rowan, sweetheart, are you alone?" my mom asked.

I groaned. "For God's sake, Mom—"

"Remember when I called and you had company! I don't know why you picked up."

I wanted to drop my phone down the nearest well. "You called me *three times.* I thought something was wrong!"

"Your voicemail wasn't working."

I could hear Dad say something to Mom, probably something along the lines of, "Why do I have to be here for this?" Dad preferred to lounge in his plush leather lounger and scroll through all the TV channels than jabber on the phone.

"Mom, I do have work this morning," I lied as I rolled back into bed. "Did you need something?"

"Is this about your friend's wedding? You know, Rowan, I'm still not sure that's a great idea," said my mom.

"So you've said. But it's happening. I'm working with their wedding planner and everything."

"Row, you seriously planning weddings now?" This was from my dad. "Is that what you left your job for?"

My dad had never understood why I'd gone into tech, and then when I'd left the industry, he'd been doubly annoyed with me. Dad had always expected that I'd take over the family business. But at the age of eighteen, I'd told Dad straight out that I had zero interest in running a bunch of hardware stores.

Dad had sold the business a year before I'd decided to quit my job. He'd never forgiven me for what he saw as a betrayal. I'd already betrayed him by getting into tech, but to quit that job and start an orange farm? It'd been too much for my old man.

"Weddings are a billion-dollar industry," I said, feeling defensive. "And the wedding planner is sure that my place could become a popular venue. It'd bring in tons of revenue. Money, Dad. Can you really look down on more money?"

"Bunch of frou-frou nonsense," Dad said. I heard him grunt, which was probably Mom smacking his arm.

"We're just worried that you're getting into something that you haven't fully researched," said Mom.

"Just trust me," I said, trying to keep the edge out of my voice. "I'm not going to screw this up."

"And you're all alone in the middle of nowhere," Mom was saying, "with nobody else. Aren't you lonely, son? Wouldn't it be better if you moved closer to your family? Your dad isn't getting any younger."

"Francie, I've hardly got one foot in the grave!" Dad griped.

"Your cholesterol is bad, and your blood pressure is high—"

I stared up at my ceiling as I listened to my parents squabble. It usually ended with Dad getting frustrated and storming off, Mom confused as to why he'd be annoyed in the first place.

"Guys, I have to get to work," I said.

"Are you seeing anybody?" Mom asked. "You know, Debra Harris's daughter—the redhead, you know?—she just got divorced. You two might hit it off. I could give you Leah's phone number."

"Mom—"

"Well, I just worry about you. I know I keep saying that,

but it's true. And it's like ever since you broke up with Melanie, you haven't even tried to date. Not really. She was the last girl you brought home." Mom's voice lowered. "Your father just left to get something to eat."

I sighed. "I just haven't had time. What with starting and running the farm, and now this wedding stuff. It's hard to meet people."

"Which just means that I think you should consider moving back home."

Considering home was a small town in the middle of nowhere near Fresno in Northern California, no fucking way. I'd left that town the day I'd graduated high school and never looked back.

"What will I do in Weston? You know there aren't any jobs there," I said.

"Well, you had a job waiting for you with your father's store."

I felt a headache coming on. "I have to go. Don't worry about me, okay?"

After we said goodbye, I lay in bed, my mind running a thousand miles per hour. I couldn't disagree with my mom: I was all alone out here. Most days, it didn't bother me. As far as dating, I had enough female company to keep me occupied.

Anna came to mind, and I turned over and punched a pillow. What the hell was Anna, then? She wasn't just a hookup now.

But was she the type of girl to take home to my parents?

She'll never let that happen. Not if it meant Melanie finding out about our relationship. That thought alone made my gut clench. It felt like a betrayal almost. Like Anna would choose her best friend over me.

Which was absurd. Anna and I, we were friends with benefits. And once this wedding business with Alejo was over, our arrangement would probably end. No feelings were involved whatsoever.

But my brain, the evil bastard, decided to provide me images of Anna with her Frat Boy Douche blind date, and it made me want to punch a hole in the wall. The thought of another man kissing her, touching her, pressing inside her tight pussy—

"Get it the fuck together," I muttered to myself.

Although I hadn't planned to do much today, I went outside and started working. Maybe with enough physical activity, this obsession with Anna Dyer could be burned out of me like the virus it was.

~

On the drive to that Saturday's wedding, Anna was uncharacteristically quiet. I had the intense urge to ask her what was wrong, but I stopped myself each time the words floated to my tongue.

We weren't in that kind of relationship. We were barely friends. Besides, she didn't need to know that I noticed when she was quiet. Maybe she just didn't feel like talking.

When we arrived at the venue that was down on the beach, Anna flinched when I took her arm. Even when she was struggling to walk in heels in the sand, she refused to let me help her.

"Is this some feminist thing, or do I have the plague?" I asked when we sat down.

Anna was a little flushed. "I can walk without assistance, thank you."

I wanted to demand to know why she was suddenly as prickly as a fucking cactus. I also wanted to rip off her dress and fuck her senseless. I wasn't entirely sure if I was just horny or genuinely concerned.

After the ceremony—which we could barely hear over the sound of the waves and the wind—we made our way to a tent for the reception. Fortunately for Anna, it wasn't on the sand.

"Ugh, walking in the sand ruined my pedicure," she moaned as she put her heels back on. "I could've sworn the invite said it was near the beach, not on it."

"Are you telling me that the great wedding planner, Anna Dyer, didn't pay attention to the mundane details of a wedding invitation?" I covered my heart in shock.

Anna glared. "Your face looks stupid when you're smug."

I helped her up, not letting her flounce off, even though I could tell by the look on her face that she wanted to.

"What bug crawled up your ass?" I hissed in her ear.

She stiffened. "Let me go—"

"Not until you tell me what's wrong. What did I do?"

"Nothing. It wasn't you."

I let her go, laughing now. "Seriously? 'It's not you, it's me'?"

"You don't have to believe me. Now, I'm going for a drink. And I'm not going to ask you if you want anything, because you're annoying me."

I watched her walk away, her ass perky as always in a satin sheath dress. Had she worn something skimpier than usual tonight? Or was it just wishful thinking?

God, I was in deep. I was in so fucking deep that I watched Anna wait in line at the open bar, and I watched in disgust as a male guest started chatting her up. When that same guest handed her her drink, like he'd paid for it despite it being an open bar, I clenched my fists.

I imagined getting up and punching that smarmy bastard in the jaw. Even worse, he was drinking a goddamn PBL. How could anyone be taken seriously when drinking warm piss beer beloved by hipsters?

"How do you know the bride and groom?" A woman sat down next to me with a warm smile. She was pretty, blond, petite. Her breasts were barely contained by her dress.

But my attention was solely on Anna. "The bride is a family friend," I replied.

"Oh, really? I know the groom." The blonde leaned closer. "He's actually my ex." She giggled. "I probably shouldn't have come, but now I'm glad that I did." She touched my arm, her long nails blood-red as she stroked my forearm.

When I saw Anna and her new boyfriend make their way to our table, I turned toward the blonde and shot her a heated smile. "I'm glad, too," I replied, my gaze fixed solely on her red, red lips.

Dinner involved Anna not looking at me as she talked with her new guy, while I did the same with my new lady. But it somehow made everything worse: I noticed every time Anna so much as shifted in her chair, or when she played with her hair. When she sighed, or laughed, or giggled, each sound sent a bolt straight to my groin.

I was tipsy by the time the dancing began. I took the blonde onto the dance floor—I'd already forgotten her name—and tried my best to forget that Anna was dancing just feet away.

"So where do you work?" the blonde asked me, snagging my attention away from the boyfriend's hand getting closer to Anna's ass.

"I grow oranges."

"What? Seriously? I love oranges. They're the best kind of orange."

I blinked. "What?"

The blonde fluttered her eyelashes. "You know, an orange is a type of orange. Just like a lime is a type of orange. Shouldn't you know something like that already?" She giggled.

I had to restrain myself from patting her on the head. "Oh, right. Of course."

"See, we're both learning all kinds of things about each other."

I grunted. My focus was solely on Anna, though, and even as ditzy as the blonde in my arms was, even she noticed my wavering attention. When I didn't even notice that a slow song had begun, my movements jerky, the blonde walked away from the floor with a huff.

And then Anna was within arm's length, her guy nowhere to be seen.

"Where's your boy?" I asked. The sounds of Ed Sheeran filled the room.

"He went to the bathroom."

Before she could walk away, I held out my hand. "Then dance with me. Just one dance."

She hesitated, but when she finally took my hand, I felt only triumph. I pulled her into my arms, our bodies in close alignment.

"Were you having fun?" I said.

Anna's lips quirked. "He stepped on my feet at least three times." She tilted her head. "How was your new friend?"

"Let's just say she's not winning a Nobel Prize any time soon."

"Rude. I'm sure she's perfectly nice."

"Oh, she was." I dipped Anna and lifted her slowly. "But she wasn't you."

Anna's eyes widened. A blush crawled up her cheeks. When my hand wandered down her back and rested in the vee of her lower back, she didn't tell me off. Instead, her blush just increased.

Dancing with Anna like this, my imagination went wild. In that moment, I imagined that we were the ones who'd just gotten married. We'd be the only two on the dance floor, the sweet notes of a love song floating around us. But we'd only have eyes, and ears, for each other.

I gazed down at her now, and my heart did that thing that scared the shit out of me. It didn't help that Anna was looking at me like I hung the moon.

I preferred her being annoyed with me. I'd rather squabble with her than discover that I couldn't imagine living without her.

The song ended abruptly, the DJ apologizing for the

hiccup. But it was like a dash of ice water had been dumped onto my head.

"Fuck, Anna," I said roughly. "What are we doing?"

She didn't say anything. She only looked like she was about to cry.

Like the fucking coward I was, I walked away, ignoring Anna calling my name.

CHAPTER FIFTEEN

ANNA

It was on a Wednesday evening that I sat down to eat dinner when I heard a knock on my door. As an antisocial millennial, I first looked through the peephole. I nearly fell over when, instead of the random stranger I was expecting, I saw Melanie.

"Are you okay?" was my greeting as I opened the door. I looked my friend over, but I didn't see any injuries.

In fact, Melanie looked fantastic. She must've gotten her hair done within the last twenty-four hours, because her blowout was pristine. Her nails were steel blue and pointed with faux diamonds at the ends. When she pushed the hair out of her face with her fancy claws, I couldn't help but think that a beautiful badger had come to my apartment.

"I'm fine!" Melanie laughed and came inside. "Why do you always assume that something's wrong?"

"Because nobody just shows up at a friend's house out of the blue?"

"You know, people used to do that all the time." Melanie

wandered into my kitchen and lifted the lid on the pot of soup I'd just made. "Ooh, I'm starving." She got out a bowl and began serving herself.

"Um, help yourself?"

I watched in confusion as Melanie doctored her soup with various toppings, humming a song under her breath. Although Melanie had always been unpredictable, she seemed almost manic right now, like her entire body was filled with electricity. It almost hurt to watch her. She opened one drawer, then another, searching for a spoon. She practically rearranged my fridge, searching for some condiments.

"What're you watching?" Melanie asked, her mouth full of soup.

"You sure you're okay?"

She patted my arm. "You're such a worrywart. Can't I spend some time with my BFF if I want to?"

Melanie settled down where I'd just been sitting. I took my soup and settled in the chair next to her. Melanie began channel surfing and eating while ignoring the elephant in the room. Namely, that she was acting like this apartment was hers and that interacting with me wasn't on the docket.

"You know, back in the day, people dropped in unannounced all the time," Melanie was saying, still changing TV channels. "People would call on each other. If the other person wasn't there, they'd leave their card."

I frowned. "Yeah, but it was at designated times. Not at eight o'clock at night."

"I wanted to see you in person." Melanie finally landed on a Spanish soap opera channel. The sounds of intense music and rapid-fire Spanish filled the living room.

"Since when do you like telenovelas?" I asked. "And since when did you speak Spanish fluently?"

"You ask way too many questions. Besides, you don't need to understand every word to know what's going on." Melanie gestured at the screen. "That woman is clearly upset with her boyfriend. He cheated on her with her best friend."

I felt my gut squeeze. "Pretty sure the woman in red just called that woman her sister."

"Whatever. Same diff." Melanie tilted her bowl back to get the rest of her soup. "Oh man, I want another bowl."

I followed her to the kitchen. When she began spooning more soup into her bowl, I grabbed the utensil and said, "What the hell is going on, Mel?"

Her grip on the spoon tightened. "I'm just hungry."

"You're acting like a crazy person. Either tell me what's going on, or go home."

Melanie replaced the serving spoon inside the pot and then slammed the lid back down, making me flinch.

"You wanna know what's going on? You have no idea?" she demanded.

"I'm not playing this game with you." Even as I said the words, I felt a chill go down my spine.

"You know, I heard from Preston that you'd canceled your date with him. I thought it was weird, because you *never* cancel. And I'd just talked to you a few days before, and I knew you weren't sick. And then when you didn't tell me you'd canceled, well, I was worried."

I sighed. "Mel—"

"And then just yesterday, Preston came into my office, all upset. He asked me why I'd set him up on a date with a woman who was already taken. I was totally lost. 'Anna? She's definitely single.'

"Then he shoved his phone in my face and showed me the pictures. You want to see them? They're kind of cute, I have to admit."

Melanie showed me the photos of me and Rowan dancing at the last wedding we'd attended. The worst one included a photo of us looking at each other like there was no one else under that tent with us.

"I couldn't believe it," said Melanie, her face turning redder with each word. "My best friend with my ex-boyfriend? The same ex I'd asked her to stay away from? No way. Not Anna. Anna would *never* betray me like that."

"How did you get those photos?" I croaked.

"A friend of a friend posted them on Instagram. Does it really matter, though? That's you, and that's Rowan."

"Mel," I said, my voice seeming to come from somebody else, "we were just dancing, at a wedding. We agreed to be each other's plus-ones because we're attending a ton of weddings lately. That's it."

I held my breath. I waited for Melanie to detect that I was lying through my teeth. When her expression changed to one of uncertainty, I felt the tension leave my body.

Melanie was staring down at her phone. Then she groaned. "Oh, Christ on a cracker, I'm an idiot."

Oh man, the guilt spiral I felt right in that moment. I felt like I was going to throw up. But I also knew that it was better this way. Melanie never needed to find out the truth. It wasn't like Rowan and I were going to end up being in an actual relationship.

Why tell Melanie we were hooking up if it was just going to upset her?

Keep justifying it if it makes you feel better, my conscience said.

Melanie then threw her arms around me and hugged me tightly. "I'm so sorry! I should never have jumped to conclusions like that. I just saw these pictures, and then you ghosted Preston, and it was like I couldn't think straight."

I patted her shoulder awkwardly. "It's okay," I soothed, my tone glum.

"But you guys seriously agreed to be each other's plus-ones?" Melanie pulled away. "Why? Do you really hate yourself that much?"

I forced out a laugh. "He's not that bad. Besides, it was just easier than going to all these weddings by myself. People get weird, you know. Trying to pair up singletons and shunting them all to the dreaded singles' table."

"People still do that?" Melanie shook her head. "That's terrible."

"You've probably never had to go to a wedding single," I said wryly.

Melanie shot me a smile. "You'd be correct." Her expression turned serious again. "I'm sorry for barging in on you like this. You probably hate me right now. I should've just called you instead of coming over like a crazy weirdo."

"Probably. You would've saved gas money, at least."

"Um, I should go, then." She glanced over her shoulder. "Shit, you didn't even get to eat, did you? I really should get out of here—"

"No, no, come on. Let's have dinner together."

I didn't know why I said that. I desperately wanted to be alone to wallow in my filthy, disgusting lies. But when Melanie brightened and seemed so happy that I didn't seem mad, I couldn't do it. I couldn't tell her to go.

And that selfish part of me, the one that felt increasingly irked that Melanie seemed to constantly win these battles of wills between us? I had to shove that part of me deep, deep down inside myself. When Melanie got shredded cheese all over the coffee table, forgot to put her glass on a coaster, and put her bowl in the sink instead of the dishwasher? I told myself it didn't matter.

I also told myself that it was punishment for lying to her in the first place.

When she hugged goodbye and I waved her off, I felt like I'd aged one hundred years. My head was starting to hurt. Or maybe it was my heart.

I had to end things with Rowan. Everything was too complicated now. I didn't do complicated. Complicated meant that I'd made mistakes, that I hadn't foreseen the storms ahead. I was the type of person to make sure the dam didn't have leaks to begin with, instead of trying to plug the leaks as they were happening.

Besides, I wasn't in love with Rowan, so breaking things off wouldn't be a big deal.

I couldn't be in love with him. I wasn't that stupid. Just because we'd hooked up didn't mean feelings had to get involved.

After I took a shower, I thought I was hallucinating when there was a knock on my door.

"Melanie, for the love of God," I said, not taking the time to look through the peephole. "What is it now. . .?"

Instead of my best friend, it was Rowan himself. And in his hands was a bouquet of flowers.

"Hi." He cleared his throat as I just stared at him. "Can I come in?"

CHAPTER SIXTEEN

ROWAN

I stood there in the hallway, holding a bouquet, like an idiot for what felt like an hour. Anna just stared at me. I stared at her. I waited for anything to happen. A piano falling on my head would've been preferable than this silence.

"Oh, for the love of God," Anna said finally. She took the flowers from me and gestured me inside. "What is it with everybody today?"

I inhaled the scents of onion and garlic. "Did you cook something?"

"Yeah, but you don't get any."

I watched as Anna searched for a vase. When she realized that the flowers were too tall, she sighed and put her head down on the counter.

I'd decided to come over on a whim. I'd seen the bouquet of flowers at the grocery store, and then I'd driven to Anna's house like we lived in a small town instead of a huge metropolitan area. I glanced at the clock on the microwave. Shit, it was nearly ten o'clock?

No wonder Anna looked more annoyed than glad to see me.

She sighed again and pulled the flowers from the vase. Without a word, I took the scissors from her and made her sit down. I began trimming the flowers, waiting for Anna to say something.

"Are you mad at me, too?" she mumbled. She looked haggard, I had to admit.

"No. I thought you'd be mad at me," I replied.

She laughed, but it held no humor in the sound. "God, we're a bunch of idiots, aren't we?" She rubbed her temples. "Melanie was just here, by the way. She found out about us."

"Okay. And?"

Anna looked annoyed now. "And now she's pissed at me and told me if I'm with you, we can't be friends."

"That's. . ." I shook my head, incredulous. "Fucking ridiculous."

"I know. It is. Yet I promised her, so I can see her side of things."

"Anna, look at me." I went to stand in front of her. With her sitting on one of her barstools, we were nearly the same height now. "Do you want me to leave?"

Anna looked sad. Then she pressed her face against my chest and replied, "No. I don't."

My heart did that stupid thing it did when I was around her. I stroked her hair, wondering if there was anything I could say to make her feel better. I had an intense urge to find Melanie and tell her to fuck off.

Anna lifted her head. "What are you thinking about?"

"What I did to Melanie to make her hate me so much."

"You don't know? Seriously?"

I shrugged. "We weren't compatible, so we broke up. We wanted different things. I knew she was hurt, but acting like this five years later. . ."

"God, men are dense." Anna rolled her eyes. "Melanie was in love with you. She thought you guys were the real deal. Then you pulled the rug out from under her feet one day, ending things. She took it hard. She's the type of person to take these kinds of things extra hard."

"She was in love with me?" I stared at Anna. "Seriously?"

"Oh, good lord. You're both idiots." She got up and stalked into her living room. "I don't have time to get in between you two."

I caught Anna by the elbow, turning her to face me. "There's no 'in between' with me and Melanie. There hasn't been in years. You know that. The only woman who I can't get out of my head lately is *you.* Why the fuck do you think I'm here right now?"

"I don't know! I don't know anything anymore. I used to know what I wanted, and who I was. But then you come around, and it's like my entire life has gone up in flames."

I had to restrain a chuckle. "I don't think it's quite that dire of a situation. Melanie will get over it. If she really cares about you, that is."

"I still feel guilty." When I snorted, Anna added, "I know it's stupid."

"It's not stupid. But you can't live your life trying to please everybody. Sometimes you have to live it without needing people's approval."

"It's not everybody's approval. I'm not that pathetic."

I kissed her forehead. "I never said you were pathetic." I kissed her nose. "I think you're amazing."

Her bottom lip quivered. "Fuck you, Rowan."

"Is that your version of 'thank you'? I feel like I need Google Translate with you."

"Maybe it just means what I said. Fuck you, Rowan, for disrupting my life like this."

I smiled. I pushed her hair over her shoulder and kissed her in a spot I knew would make her moan. "You're welcome."

I inhaled the scent of her skin. She must've just gotten out of the shower, because her hair was wet along her hairline. She also smelled like soap, and it made me want to lick her from head to toe.

This version of Anna was soft and warm. She wasn't all dolled up in her wedding clothes, every hair on her head in the right spot. She was wearing a ratty T-shirt and shorts and, to my delight, no bra.

"I'll ask you one last time," I said into her ear, "do you want me to leave?"

She wrinkled her nose. "I already told you: stay. I want you to stay."

She wrapped her arms around my neck and pulled me down for a kiss. I molded my body to hers as I licked inside her luscious mouth.

"I took a Plan B," she said at the same moment I tossed her T-shirt over her head.

It took my brain a moment to process what she'd said. "Okay. Thanks." I cupped her breasts and flicked her nipples with my nails.

Anna sucked in a breath. "Did you bring condoms this time?"

"I thought you'd have some." When she froze, I laughed. "I'm kidding, babe." I pulled a bunch of condoms from my pocket, flashing them like they were a bunch of cash. "We're good to go."

"How many times do you think we'll have sex? You know what, never mind."

We made it to Anna's bedroom, undressing each other slowly. I massaged her shoulders while she scratched her nails across my scalp. I felt goosebumps rise on my arms. When Anna went down on her knees in front of me, the goosebumps only increased.

She licked her lips as she stroked my cock. It didn't take long for me to become fully hard. When she enveloped the head inside her mouth, I groaned aloud.

She sucked and licked my cock, the sounds making an erotic soundtrack. With her gazing up at me under her lashes, her lips red as she blew me, I felt like the luckiest guy in the entire fucking world.

Anna fondled my balls at the same time she licked me from root to tip. "I kinda want to keep going until you come in my mouth," she said.

Her words made me shudder. "Fuck me, baby. I'm tempted to let you."

She smiled. Then she took me until the tip of my cock bumped the back of her throat. I dug my fingers into her hair, gently helping her bob up and down my length. My toes curled into her rug as I felt my balls draw up into my body.

"Fuck," I said, helping her up. I kissed her hard. "You're way too good at that."

She laughed. "Glad you enjoyed yourself."

I moved us so we were on the bed. The condoms I'd brought were scattered across the comforter like metallic rose petals. I covered Anna, loving the way our bodies melded together. I grabbed one of the condoms, sheathing my cock, Anna's eyes heavy-lidded and heated as she watched me.

"Spread your legs," I said, nearly growling.

Anna smiled and slowly complied. Heat rose in my cheeks. Her pussy was already soaked. My mouth watered. The memory of eating her out made me shudder.

"Rowan." Anna's tone was pleading. She arched her hips. "Touch me."

"Where, baby? Tell me where you want me."

She whimpered. Spreading her pussy lips, she said, "Right here."

I didn't need to be told twice. I licked her from top to bottom, feeling her fingers quivering. I sank my tongue inside her as I began rubbing her clit with light strokes.

Anna grabbed at my hair, her grip getting tighter with every lick and kiss. Her wetness covered my chin; it only egged me on and made me want to bring her to orgasm.

But just as I felt her about to come, she sat up, closing her legs. "I need you," she said. Her cheeks were flushed, and her nipples were rigid.

I squeezed the base of my cock. Seeing her in bed, her hair messy, her body sweaty and red, her gaze desperate for me to fuck her? It was enough to make me come right then and there.

"Get on your back," I commanded. When she did as I said, I nearly groaned aloud.

I pushed my cock deep inside her pussy in a single stroke. Anna cried out. Entangling our hands together, I rode her until she was incoherent under me. I could feel her pussy grip me, tighter and tighter, just like her fingers had gripped my hair.

"Keep going, keep going," she was muttering into my ear. "Just like that— Oh my God!"

I grinned. I did as she asked, and when she came, she shouted her release right in my ear. The feeling of her pulsing around me sent me straight into my orgasm. I came with a long, low groan, my cock pulsing inside her for what felt like eternity.

We collapsed into a tangled heap of sweaty, sated limbs. Anna pushed her hair from her face, panting, while I struggled to catch my own breath. As I rubbed Anna's back, I felt her shudder with aftershocks.

"Jesus Christ," Anna said, shaking her head. "I think that was better even than last time."

I laughed. "You think? It definitely was."

Her eyes were wide now, and I watched as something crossed her face. She shook her head, burying her face in my shoulder.

"Can we cuddle?" Her voice was small, unsure.

I gently combed my fingers through her hair. "Isn't that what we're doing?"

She sighed. I let my body go slack, and before I realized it, I fell into a deep sleep.

CHAPTER SEVENTEEN

ANNA

Rowan and I didn't see each other for nearly two weeks after that. He texted nearly every day; I responded in kind. But I never initiated communication, unless it was about Emily and Alejo's wedding.

I was being a coward. I was avoiding both the man I'd fallen in love with and my best friend. I didn't know how to face either of them.

So I threw myself into my work. That was what I always did when relationships got sticky. I avoided the things that made me uncomfortable. I figured that Melanie would cool off and that Rowan would get bored with me. Then we could all go back to how things were.

Despite my best efforts, though, it was nearly impossible to stop thinking about Rowan. When I'd see a tall guy with broad shoulders and a similar hair color on the street, my heart would skip a beat. This meant I was basically going into cardiac arrest every time I stepped outside my home, considering how many men like Rowan lived in the area.

And even if I managed not to think about him during

the day, my dreams were so lurid that I'd wake up with my pussy throbbing. I'd give in and reach for my vibrator to finish myself off.

It was on a hot, but windy, Monday that Emily came to my office. She arrived ten minutes early, forcing me to down my latte before it got cold. Emily's expression was uncharacteristically strained. I'd never seen her without a bright smile on her face.

"Is Alejo coming?" I asked.

Emily's lips thinned. "No. He's busy."

"No worries." I forced myself to sound peppy. "I wanted to follow up with you on our last email. I put together a list of DJs for you and Alejo to look through whenever you get a chance—"

"Alejo doesn't want a DJ. He thinks we should get a band. He mentioned that to you, remember?"

Uh, no? But I smiled brightly anyway. "Did he? Well, I can put together another list for you guys. Just a note that a full band will probably be twice the price that a DJ would be—"

"Alejo keeps saying that we're spending too much money, so it can't be expensive." Emily looked aggrieved. "Our parents have already given us so much money for this wedding, but it's not enough. It keeps getting bigger, and the budget keeps going up."

She looked like she was about to burst into tears. When she started sniffling, I handed her a box of tissues. It wasn't the first time a bride or groom had cried in my office, and it probably wouldn't be the last.

"I think he wants to call off the wedding," Emily said, tears falling down her cheeks now.

"Did he say that?"

"No, no. But he won't make up his mind about anything, and then he gets frustrated when I ask him his opinion. And then like with the DJ, suddenly he wants a fucking band?" Emily shook her head and sobbed.

"Weddings are often really stressful. If there's anything I can do for you guys. . ."

Emily was tearing the tissue into smaller and smaller bits. She kept shaking her head at me.

Then, she asked: "Did you call the winery? The one in Santa Barbara?"

A vague memory of Emily asking me that floated into my brain. "Crap, I don't think I did. I'll get right on that." I scribbled a note to myself and then underlined the words five times.

"You didn't call? Because they told me I had to book them by the beginning of May, before they raise their prices. We had to order bottles at their original price because otherwise we'd go way over budget—" Emily's voice rose in octave with every word.

"It'll be fine. I'll explain things, let them know I dropped the ball."

"We have to have wine from that vineyard! It's Alejo's favorite! He proposed there!"

"Emily, take a deep breath for me—"

"No, I will not take a deep breath." She stood up, the torn-up tissue falling to the floor like confetti. "This is a huge deal. And you know what else? It takes you days to respond to an email. And when you do respond, you don't even answer all my questions. And where's the list of catering vendors? You've never sent me that. I've already asked you twice."

I felt like she'd reached across my desk and slapped me. I swallowed the defensive retort on my tongue.

"Emily, I'm sorry," I said. "How about we table this discussion until we're both calmer? Then we can figure out how to move forward."

"Now you're acting like I'm crazy." Emily's eyes filled with tears again. "I don't need this. I don't need any of this bullshit!"

Emily left, the front door to the office suite slamming closed. I stared down at my desk in shock.

Had I really dropped the ball this badly? I *never* fucked up like this. But I couldn't remember Emily asking about caterers twice. And as far as I knew, I'd always replied to her emails promptly.

I went through my inbox, reading every one of Emily's emails and going over every single one of my replies. I winced when I realized that in the last three weeks, I hadn't been replying promptly. And in more than one email, I'd missed one or two of Emily's questions.

It wasn't dire, by any means. We had nearly ten more months to go. But I had a feeling that Alejo's sudden cold feet and my sloppy work had combined to make Emily freak out like she had.

I sent Emily an apologetic email. I considered also calling her, but I had a feeling I wasn't at the top of her list of people she wanted to talk to.

I wiped the sweat from my forehead. I felt shaky and anxious. I knew that, logically, this was fixable. I knew that, but it didn't help me feel calmer.

I'd fucked up. Worse, I'd fucked up because I'd let myself get distracted by Rowan Caldwell.

I had never, in my entire life, let a man take over my brain space like Rowan had. Hell, with my last boyfriend, he'd gotten pissed when I'd chosen my work over our relationship—or at least, that was why he'd broken up with me.

I'd met Jason at a wedding. He'd been one of the groomsmen, and he'd been charming and flirtatious all evening. I'd just started my wedding planning business, and when I'd told Jason all about it, he'd seemed impressed.

But as the months went by, our relationship had quickly progressed from seeing each other at least twice a week, to seeing each other only on the weekend. The space in between our meetings lengthened as business picked up. More than once, I'd had to cancel on Jason when a wedding went long. At that point, I hadn't yet figured out the art of managing a bridal party's time.

When we met for brunch one hot, June morning, Jason only ordered coffee and nothing else. That should've been my clue that something was up. But I was oblivious. As far as I knew, everybody was happy.

"My mom is coming up to visit next week," Jason said. "She wants to meet you."

"Next weekend? I have a wedding. It's wedding season, you know that." I smiled and squeezed his hand. "She just lives in San Diego, right? Maybe we can go down there to see her later in the year."

Jason looked annoyed. "We tried that over the holidays. You had weddings."

Our waiter set a plate of waffles in front of me, distracting me entirely from what was right in front of me.

"Hopefully this year I can make it down there with you," I said.

"Anna, this isn't working."

"What? The coffee?"

Jason scowled. "Seriously?"

"Now I'm lost."

"You know what? Now I'm really done. If you want a relationship, you have to show up. You're barely around lately. I never see you. You take forever to reply to my texts. I'm not going to beg you to be with me." His lip curled. "I have other options."

"Is that code for 'I'm cheating on you'?" Now I was outraged. "Because if you were really unhappy, you could've said something before now."

"What's the point? You'd tell me you're busy and maybe we could talk about it next week." Jason laid down a few dollar bills. "I'm out. Enjoy your weddings, Anna."

I considered going after him, but then I looked at my plate of waffles and figured that eating them would be more worthwhile. Anger rumbled in my gut: not just at Jason, but also at myself. I'd been so laser-focused on my business that my relationship had been imploding under my nose. Then again, Jason hadn't exactly tried to communicate with me.

"Fuck you, Jason," I muttered as I speared my last bite of waffle. He'd probably been cheating on me for months.

That realization hurt. He should've broken up with me ages ago, but instead, he'd probably gone behind my back in the hopes that I'd notice and want him to come back to me.

I'd barely dated much after Jason. I'd had my business, and then I'd bought a house, and then when I began working as a bridesmaid-for-hire, I'd had zero time for a social life.

But sitting here in my office, feeling guilty about how I'd been handling Emily and Alejo's wedding, I felt like a failure. And it also showed me that my initial instinct to stay far away from Rowan had been right.

Was I really going to throw away my business for a guy who probably didn't see me as more than a fling? I was smarter than that. And if being ambitious and capable meant that I had to be single forever, well, I'd deal with it.

Or maybe you're just afraid Rowan would leave you like Jason had. Yeah, maybe that was my fear. That once again, I'd make another man unhappy and he'd end up telling me to go to hell. While I was left holding the buck, wondering what I'd done wrong besides pursue my dreams.

CHAPTER EIGHTEEN

ROWAN

Alejo arrived a half hour late to the bar. He had never been the most punctual guy, but a half hour late was beyond even his standard. When he sat down next to me at the bar, he looked like he'd been run over by a truck. I half-wondered if he was already drunk.

"You okay, man?" I asked.

Alejo grunted a non-answer. He ordered a beer and then proceeded to stare at his hands morosely.

Considering Alejo had been the one to text me to get drinks, I was tempted to tell him we should reschedule. But when his shoulders slumped and he sighed like a heartsick middle schooler, I knew I couldn't bail. No matter how uncomfortable it all made me.

"I think we're calling off the wedding," Alejo said.

Out of all the things I expected my friend to say, it wasn't that. "Seriously?"

"I don't know. Maybe." Alejo rubbed his hands through his hair, disheveling it further. "Em and I got into a fight last night. She sent over a bill for something—I don't fucking remember what it was—and I freaked out. The wedding keeps getting more and more expensive. Why the fuck are we paying ten grand for a photographer?"

Alejo's eyes were wild now. He barely noticed when the bartender placed his beer in front of him.

"Who said they wanted to cancel?" I asked. Internally, I was selfishly thinking, *Do I have to return their deposit now?* I could just see Anna scowling at me for that thought. And maybe slapping me upside the head for good measure.

"I did." Alejo winced. "It was in the heat of the moment. Things have been stressful. Em's mom is helping pay for the wedding, but she keeps wanting to invite everybody and their dog. So that means catering will be more expensive.

"Now Em is freaking out, since she's not sure if our venue"—Alejo let out a sad laugh—"I mean, your place, can fit three hundred people."

"Three hundred people! You said maybe one hundred!"

"That's what I told Em." Alejo finally drank his beer, staring at the condensation dripping down the sides of the glass. "She told me I wasn't listening to her and I've barely helped her with the wedding. Which is a lie, because she won't *let* me help. I give my opinion, but she just goes with what she wants."

I grimaced. I also had no idea what to tell Alejo. I was hardly Dr. Phil with the deep life advice.

"Sorry to hear that," was my lame reply.

Alejo chuckled. "Shit, you're terrible at this. Remind me not to come to you for relationship advice."

Even though he was right, I still felt a prick of annoyance. I wasn't a complete fucking moron.

"Speaking of which. . ." Alejo's gaze slid toward mine. "We couldn't help but notice that you and Anna were acting weird around each other."

Christ, I did not want to talk about Anna. "You're seeing things," I replied.

"No way. I saw it, and so did Em. We thought you guys were going to bang it out right there in the middle of your farm."

I shot Alejo a warning look. "Once again: it's none of your business."

"Shit, I was right. There is something between you two. 'None of your business' is always code for 'we're fucking.'"

"Since when did you turn into a teenage girl obsessed with gossip?"

He shrugged. "Since my life is in flames, I have to distract myself. Making you squirm is fun."

I scowled. "We're just friends."

"Yet you've been each other's plus-ones for a bunch of weddings now. Yeah, I heard through the grapevine. We run in the same circles. And a little bird told me that you guys were oblivious to anyone else at the last wedding you were at."

"Do you guys seriously gossip at the office about this shit?"

Alejo shrugged. "If you hadn't left, you could give your side of the story."

I just snorted.

We drank our beers in silence. I was tempted to press Alejo further about his fight with Emily, if it meant getting him off my own back.

"You could still come back, you know," said Alejo.

"In case you forgot, you're supposed to get married on *my* property."

At Alejo's wince, guilt struck me. "Sorry. Ignore me. But I have no interest in selling my farm."

"Maybe you could return part-time. We could really use you." Alejo held up a hand. "I know what you'll say. Just know that the offer still stands. And maybe things will change. Maybe you won't want to live in the middle of nowhere for the rest of your life, if something else works out for you."

"What, now you're basically planning my wedding?" I scoffed.

Despite my best efforts, I couldn't help but wonder if Anna would be willing to move to my place. If we got together, that is. Or would she insist on me moving in with her? Could I maintain the farm that way? I'd have to hire someone to manage things day-to-day. I was already planning to do that, though, if the wedding-venue plan bore fruit.

"I might not be the best person to listen to right now," Alejo said quietly, "but if you really care about Anna, tell her. Your pride isn't worth keeping your mouth shut."

"Like I said: there's nothing between us." *Nothing that I want to admit to.*

"I've known you for seven years, and I've never seen you act this way around a woman. Getting all cagey and weird. And you couldn't keep your eyes off her at the farm. Like I wasn't even sure you heard a word I said that day. And now you guys are going to weddings together—"

I finished off my beer in one long gulp. "I need more booze if we're going to keep talking about this shit."

Fortunately for me, Alejo agreed. We were soon four beers deep, and the mood had lightened considerably. When we got up to play a round of darts, Alejo staggered, forcing me to catch him before he fell.

"When did you get to be such a damn lightweight?" I asked.

"Em doesn't like to drink." Alejo burped. "So I stopped drinking as much."

"And you want to get married, why?" I threw a dart, which just hit the edge of the board. "Sounds like a shitty deal to me. You have to spend tens of thousands on a wedding you don't want, you can't have fun anymore, you don't get to go out, especially if you have kids. . ."

"It's not that simple." Alejo's throw was so far off that it hit the wall with a loud thunk. "I love her."

I raised an eyebrow. "You sound miserable, dude."

"Because she's mad at me." Alejo rubbed his face, but not before I took the dart in his hand away from him so he didn't poke himself in the eye. "And I didn't mean what I said. About canceling the wedding. I just got frustrated."

I threw my next dart. Almost a bullseye. "Then you should go home and tell her."

"She told me she didn't want to see me," Alejo mumbled.

"What, did she change the locks? Just go home. Get on your knees and beg for forgiveness if you have to."

"She was really pissed at me." Alejo looked so pathetic I nearly gave him a hug in the middle of the fucking bar.

"Yeah, and? Didn't you just tell me not to let your pride get in your way?"

Alejo and I kept drinking, until I finally forced him into

a cab to go home. He looked so grateful that I'd ordered him a ride that he looked like he was about to burst into tears.

"Rowan," he said, his words slurring, "I love ya, man."

I patted his back awkwardly. "Love you, too. But you should really go tell Emily that. Although maybe sober up a bit first."

"She probably will make me sleep outside." Alejo laughed. "It'll be fun. I haven't gone camping in foreveeeeeer." Then his gaze fastened on me. "Tell Anna how you feel. Don't keep saying it's nothin'. It's somethin'. I know it. I've seen it before. Nothin' is just nothin'. Ya know?"

"Sure, buddy. Come on, let's get you inside the car."

Alejo waved exuberantly as the cab drove off. I hoped that the drive would sober him up a bit. It was at least thirty minutes to his place, an hour if you were especially unlucky.

For myself, I was tipsy but not sloshed. I considered either getting something to eat to sober up, or to continue drinking.

So I kept drinking. I ended up playing darts with a few other regulars. Jerry, who could drink anybody under the table, had probably consumed an entire bottle of whiskey by midnight and was still coherent. As for me, I was confused as to why my throws were so wildly off each and every time.

When my last throw nearly hit some poor schlub coming from the bathroom, Jerry took the remaining dart from me.

"That's it for tonight, son. You got a ride home?"

"Yeah. My truck. It's out there." I gestured vaguely.

"You ain't driving nowhere. Not like this. You want something to eat?" Jerry didn't wait for my answer. Instead, he went to order something greasy from the bar.

I pulled out my phone, scrolling mindlessly. I checked my email inbox: nothing. And Anna hadn't texted me, either. Apparently I was just a booty call for her. Except this round, I'd shown up at her door like a sad puppy that had gotten caught in the rain.

u up, I texted her. It took me an absurd amount of time to type those three letters. It didn't help that I couldn't remember how to correctly spell *you* in my drunken haze.

No answer. Was she asleep? It wasn't that late.

hey

hey

u up ?

Im drunk lolol

Anna replied with just a question mark. And then: *have you been hacked?*

I laughed aloud. When Jerry returned, I showed him Anna's message. "I haven't been hacked, though. It's me. Messaging *her*. Ha, ha, ha."

Jerry frowned down at me. "Son, unless that's your wife, you better snap out of it. Nothing good ever came out of bugging a woman when you're drunk."

"She's not my wife." I frowned down at my phone. "She doesn't like me like that."

Right then, Anna replied, *Rowan? You there?*

I slowly typed the words, *I miss u wanna see u.*

Then, silence. When Jerry pushed a burger and fries toward me, I barely noticed the food. I was solely focused on Anna replying.

We should talk, was her only reply.

When I hit the button to call her, Jerry snatched the phone from my hand. "You'll get this back when you're done eating. Eat!"

I ate. Jerry seemed like the type of guy to force-feed me if necessary. Besides, I actually was hungry. I hadn't eaten much since this morning.

But after eating and while Jerry was in the bathroom, I took my phone back. Anna hadn't replied again. Drunk, stupid, desperate, I texted the words that would seal my doom.

I think I love u.

Jerry helped me get a motel room across the street to sleep off the booze. Mostly because I really didn't want to leave my truck unattended until God knows when.

"Don't sleep with the comforter," Jerry advised. "They never wash those. And don't use the coffee pot. Speak from experience. Nearly blew up my own toilet after a mishap in 1996."

I'd lain down, mostly because I felt dizzy and rather like I could throw up if I weren't careful. I waved a hand.

"Get some sleep. And don't text that girl again."

"Duh."

Then I was snoring, completely oblivious to what would await me in the morning.

CHAPTER NINETEEN

ANNA

One of my fellow bridesmaids pushed a mimosa into my hands with a bright smile. "You've barely had anything!"

After she left to attend to her hair, I set the mimosa aside. Considering I was the bridesmaid-for-hire for this wedding, I could hardly get drunk off my ass before the ceremony had even started.

The bride, Mia, apparently hadn't gotten that memo. She'd been downing mimosas all morning. At the moment, she was laughing and gesturing wildly at the mirror.

I sighed inwardly. Mia had seemed so calm, even shy, during all of our conversations. Her fiancé Jackson had been the one who'd spoken the most. It had almost seemed that Mia hadn't even been interested in wedding planning.

I checked my phone. We had an hour until the ceremony. We'd just finished taking photos, and now the wedding parties—separated by gender—were hiding out until the ceremony began.

"Shots, shots, shots!" The bridesmaid who'd handed me

the mimosa came bearing a tray of shots, walking unsteadily toward Mia.

I stepped in front of the bridesmaid's path. What was her name again? Jenny? "I think the bride has had enough. We want her to get down the aisle, right?"

Jenny made a face. "She's fine. Mia, aren't you good?"

Mia mumbled something unintelligible. Looking at her red cheeks and the snot running down her face, she was hardly the epitome of *good.*

I snagged the tray from Jenny. "Let's save these for cocktail hour. I'll have the caterer put them in the fridge."

Jenny just sighed, like I was the worst person alive.

I sneaked out of the barn-like structure where the bridal party was hanging out and quickly disposed of the shots in the trash. Maybe it was petty, but I didn't want any of these people to get their hands on any more booze.

By the time the ceremony began, Mia was shaking like a leaf. Worse, she vomited right as the procession was starting.

I handed her a bottle of water. "We can delay things," I whispered, wiping her forehead. "Do you want me to get Jackson?"

Mia kept waving her hands. "No, no, no, I'm fine, let's get this over with." She sounded annoyed that I'd even suggest such a thing.

And so I watched from the front of aisle with the rest of the wedding party, my fingers crossed that Mia would make it down the aisle. It didn't help that she'd planned to walk herself. If she had her dad around, at least I could be assured she wasn't going to run. Or lock herself in the bathroom, puking.

I caught Rowan's eye. He shot me a smile, but it was

halfhearted. I wished I'd dumped that tray of shots on his head now.

Speaking of drunken shenanigans. . . After getting those texts from Rowan, I'd freaked out. When I'd called him the next morning, he'd grumpily replied that he'd been drunk, he hadn't meant it, and that I shouldn't worry about it.

The guy I've caught feelings for might love me but refuses to be honest about it. Yeah, that's not anxiety-inducing at all.

The music for the bride's entrance began. I waited with bated breath. I caught Jenny covering her mouth to hide a smirk.

The music continued; the bride, however, remained elusive. Jackson shot me a glance.

As I was about to go find out what was going on, Mia finally appeared. Her bouquet looked half-smashed, and her train was rumpled despite me fluffing it out right before the ceremony had begun.

Mia stopped at the end of the aisle, staring wildly, like she'd forgotten what she was supposed to do. The musicians, bless them, returned to the beginning of the song and began playing it more slowly.

"Come on, come on," I said under my breath. "Please, Mia."

Mia took a deep breath. Then she began walking—quickly. She nearly sprinted down the aisle, the musicians having to pick up speed. By the time she reached Jackson and handed me her pathetic-looking bouquet, I could see the musicians were wiping sweat from their foreheads.

I fluffed Mia's train once again, feeling sweat drip down my face. It didn't help that it was an outdoor ceremony, and it was a hot day. Worse, the ceremony went on, and on, and on, and everyone was in full sun with no parasols or fans in sight.

I breathed a sigh of relief when Jackson and Mia said their vows and began placing the rings on each other's fingers. The officiant pronounced them husband and wife, and everyone erupted in a cheer, probably from sheer relief that the damn ceremony was over.

Jackson dipped Mia over his arm to kiss her. But she wasn't expecting that move, because she flailed in his arms. In her attempt to right herself, she hit Jackson in the face. He let out a yelp and dropped his new wife straight to the ground in a heap of white satin.

"What the fuck!" Jackson rubbed his nose. Blood was now pouring down his face.

I rushed to help Mia. Lifting her up, she groaned and muttered that she was going to be sick.

"Shit." I grabbed one of the vases, dumped the poor flowers out, and then handed the container to Mia just in the nick of time. She puked with gusto as all her guests watched in horror.

Jackson's mom was helping him tip his head back, mopping the blood from his face, saying over and over again, "My baby, my poor baby!"

It was total chaos. It was only by the grace of God that I managed to get Mia back to the bridal suite. Returning to the guests, I announced in my cheeriest voice, "Cocktail hour starts now over by the entrance!"

As the guests began to make their way toward sustenance, I heard Rowan say over my shoulder, "Here."

He handed me a cup of water. I gulped it down, and he refilled it without saying another word.

"From a scale of one to ten being dead doves," said Rowan, "what would you rate this ceremony?"

I glared at him, then considered his question. "An eight. Only because no one died."

His lips quirked. "A ten includes death? Do you have any examples?"

"No, and I hope I never do. Although I did attend one where one of the uncles had a heart attack mid-dance. Apparently he'd taken a little too much Viagra that night in hopes of scoring with one of the bridesmaids."

Rowan rubbed my shoulder. "Come on. You need food."

"After listening to Mia vomit? No, thanks. Just booze for me."

Mia and Jackson reappeared for the reception. To my surprise, their entrance was exuberant, Mia looking like nothing had happened. If not for Jackson's swollen nose, you'd never have known it had been anything other than a normal ceremony.

Although I was supposed to sit next to Mia, somehow Jenny finagled things so that I was sitting at the end of the table. I had a feeling Jenny was salty that she hadn't been asked to be the maid of honor, never knowing that I'd literally been hired for the job.

I was ignored for most of dinner. I took it in stride, trying to make conversation but not forcing things, either. By the time we got to the entree, Rowan came up to me and told me to come with him.

"Nobody puts baby in a corner," he quoted.

I laughed. I took my plate of food and followed him. No

one in the wedding party said a thing at my departure. Besides, I'd done my job. Now it was time to eat and party.

"I wasn't in the corner," I told him as I sat down next to him.

"The point still stands. Besides, aren't you the maid of honor? Shouldn't you be next to the bride?"

I shrugged. "Not according to her BFF."

We watched as Jenny lowered her head next to Mia. Jackson himself seemed more interested in his plate of food than in his new wife.

"Do you ever do weddings where you know they're not going to last?" asked Rowan.

"It's not my place to assess that."

"Oh, come on." He gestured toward the newly married couple. "How long do you give them? A year?"

"Nah." I shrugged a shoulder. "Probably three. They'll have a kid or two, he'll have an affair, then she'll leave and take him for everything. It's a classic story."

"And here I thought I was the cynical one."

"Not cynical. Just realistic."

When the dancing started, I went to the bathroom and ended up outside in the nearby garden. I rubbed my arms at the chill. I should go back inside, in case Mia needed something. But instead, I stared up at the moon and enjoyed the brief respite from the crowd.

"I wondered where you'd gone," said Rowan. I felt him place his jacket over my shoulders. "You'll freeze out here."

I glanced down at my skimpy bridesmaid dress made of only satin and a few thin straps. "It's nice out," I said.

I could feel Rowan gazing down at me. When I turned

my head slightly, I felt the impact of his eyes throughout the entirety of my body.

It didn't help that, framed in moonlight, he was even more handsome than usual. It also reminded me of our first meeting that night at Trevor and Meredith's wedding. That night, I'd wanted him to kiss me.

This night, he actually did.

He enveloped me in a kiss that made me moan against his lips. His hands were everywhere: my back, my shoulders, my ass. I wanted to crawl inside him and never leave. It was such a strange, desperate feeling that I felt unmoored.

"Anna?" His voice was gruff in my ear.

"I kept telling myself I had to stay away from you. That this would never work." I touched his cheek. "But I just can't seem to do it. In my entire life, I've never once not had the willpower to do something. But you make me weak."

His forehead crinkled. "Does that make you weak? Because then I'm weak, too." He brushed his thumb across my lower lip. "And if you think you could've gotten rid of me, you're wrong. I would've found you, no matter where you went."

I kissed him this time. I stood on tiptoes, even wearing heels, dragging my fingers through his hair to hear him groan. When I scratched his scalp, I felt him shiver.

I wasn't sure how we ended up on a nearby bench. But suddenly I was on Rowan's lap, and he was sucking and licking the side of my neck. The wedding, the sounds of people talking, the music playing, it all faded away.

Rowan cupped my breasts, flicking my nipples. "No bra?" he said. "Dirty girl."

"Can't wear one," I said breathily, "with this dress."

"I'm going to tell myself you did it for me."

"I'm not wearing panties, either."

Rowan groaned. His hand found the slit of my dress, slowly dragging his fingers along the inside of my thigh. I shuddered. He kneaded the flesh there, his other hand holding me steady so he could keep kissing me.

"Anna, open your eyes."

I held his gaze as he parted my pussy lips. When he dragged a knuckle from top to bottom of my slit, I felt like I could explode right then and there.

"Damn, baby, you're gorgeous." He pressed his forehead to mine as he gently pushed a finger inside me, his thumb rubbing my clit. "I bet I could make you come real quick. I can already feel you getting tighter. If I'd known you were this horny, I would've fucked you before we got here."

I couldn't speak. I could only hold on to Rowan's shoulders as he finger-fucked me. I knew we were playing with fire. I knew we could be caught at any moment.

I knew those things, but at that moment, I didn't care.

Rowan pushed another finger inside my dripping pussy. I cried out, burying my face in his shoulder. As he kept fucking me with his hands, his fingers playing me like a musical instrument, my belly tightened with my impending orgasm.

"I wonder what'll happen if I do this. . ." Rowan pressed upward inside me and rubbed me harder.

My eyes flew open. I was gasping for breath. I couldn't move. I could only feel the exquisite pleasure of Rowan making me come. I was nearly there; I could taste the orgasm on my tongue.

That was when I heard a woman cry out. I was shoved

behind Rowan before he stood up. It took me a long second to realize that somebody had found our hiding spot.

"Oh my God," the voice said.

I froze at the sound. I knew that voice. It couldn't be—

"Rowan?" Melanie stepped closer. "Sorry to interrupt, I thought. . ."

I stood up. Although it was dark out here, there was enough light from both the reception tent and the moon to illuminate our trio of faces.

Melanie's eyes widened. "What is this?"

CHAPTER TWENTY

ANNA

Why was Melanie here? And how had I not noticed her earlier? I'd even printed out the seating chart, and Melanie hadn't been on the list. I would've noticed that, surely?

"Mel—" I said, stepping toward her.

"I knew it. I knew you guys were fucking around." Melanie was shaking her head. Her gaze collided with mine. "You lied to me. I can't believe it." She turned and walked away.

"Shit." I glanced at Rowan, whose expression was grave. "I have to go after her."

Melanie was nearly running by the time I caught up with her. "Mel, I'm so sorry," was all I could think to say as I grabbed her arm.

She jerked away from me, her eyes wild now. "Did you sleep with him?" she demanded. Then she laughed darkly. "That's a stupid question. You were about to have sex on that fucking bench! No, my real question is: how long has this been going on?"

I said nothing. I didn't have to. The look on my face said everything, I was sure.

"Oh my God," Melanie said. "Oh my God."

"I didn't mean for this to happen—"

"Jesus Christ! How could you?" Now Melanie was crying, and it made me feel like the biggest piece of shit alive. "Why? When I asked you not to?"

"It just happened," I repeated.

"It just happened? What, you fell down straight onto Rowan's dick?" Her tone was scathing.

Although I had the strong urge to beg for forgiveness, the other part of me felt only anger. "Look, I'm sorry I broke my promise. I'm not proud of that. But I should never have promised you that to begin with. You and Rowan haven't dated in five years. Why do you get to claim him? Why tell me I'm not 'allowed' to date him?"

Melanie stared at me. "I never said you weren't allowed—"

"That's exactly what you said!"

Melanie's tears increased. "You don't get it. He broke my heart. I don't think you know how much. The thought of you together. . . It would mean we couldn't be friends. Because I don't think I could stand being around *him*."

I gaped at my best friend. "You'd seriously end our friendship because of Rowan. Because I wanted to date him."

"I don't want to end things! But I'd have to! For my own mental health. The thought of being around him, I couldn't stand it. It'd just constantly remind me of what he did."

"Jesus, what did he do?" I felt like I was going to vomit. "Is there something you're not telling me?"

Melanie just looked sad. "No. I've already told you what happened. I put my all into that relationship, while he slowly went ice-cold. Then he left me without a second look back. I'd truly thought we'd end up getting engaged. Married. The whole nine yards. But it was like I was an afterthought to him. I think I was actually an afterthought the entire relationship."

I sighed. "I'm sorry. That would hurt anybody. But you have to let go of this resentment, anger, sadness, whatever it is. It's been five years."

"And I thought I had, until he came back into our lives!" Melanie swiped at her eyes. "And when I asked you to do one thing, you couldn't do it. I never thought you'd choose a guy over our friendship. Are you in love with him? Because let me tell you, he'll make you regret it. You can give him your heart, but Rowan Caldwell will stomp all over it without breaking a sweat."

When I said nothing, Melanie repeated, "Are you, then? In love with him?"

I licked my lips. "No. It's just a fling." Even as I said the words, I felt my palms grow damp and my head started spinning.

"Damn, Anna, since when did you become a liar? Come on, be honest with me. You love him. Or at the very least, you love him fucking you. Is the dick worth it? To betray our friendship for a man?"

"I'm sorry I lied. I am. I should've been honest with you. But I also knew you'd freak out. Because everything has to be about you, right?"

My voice got louder with each word. "It's always about how *you* feel. How something will affect *you.* I've lived my life trying to regulate your feelings, and you know what? I'm not going to do that anymore. If I want to fuck each and every one of your ex-boyfriends, I will."

Melanie was pale now. "This isn't you. What happened to you?"

"Rowan happened to me. I fell in love with him." *There, I said the words aloud.* "And I'm not going to apologize for that."

"Woooooow." Melanie shook her head, laughing a little. "You can't be serious. You fell for him? Oh, sweetheart. No."

I flinched. I had the sudden urge to scratch out her eyeballs. She looked so smug now.

"Look, I've been there. I fell for his bullshit, too. I get it." Melanie touched my arm, squeezing it a little too hard. "He'll say all the right things. He's great in bed. But the second you're looking for commitment, guess what's gonna happen?"

I swallowed. My throat felt dry. "You're projecting."

Melanie shrugged. "Tell him. See what he does. And when he goes ice-cold on you and then basically disappears one day? Don't say that I didn't warn you."

"You're being deliberately cruel now."

"Oh, come on! Pot, meet kettle. You lied straight to my face multiple times. You made a promise and then you broke it, over and over again. Did you think about that when you guys were fucking?"

I pushed her hand aside. "That's enough. I don't have to listen to this."

But apparently, Melanie wasn't done. "I'm saying this for your own good. I don't want you to get hurt."

"This has long gone way past you wanting to protect me. Even if Rowan does hurt me, so what? That's my burden to bear. You don't get to control me."

To my chagrin, Melanie's eyes filled with tears. I wanted to hug her, but I resisted. This wasn't something we could just resolve with a hug and a trip to our favorite dive bar for drinks to hash things out.

"I'm going back to the wedding," I said. "Don't talk to me again."

ON THE DRIVE back to my house, Rowan said little. I had nothing to say. I was too tired to explain, anyway.

I didn't even notice when he'd stopped his truck in front of my house.

"Anna," he said softly. He touched my hand.

I hurried out of the truck and went inside without even saying goodbye. To my frustration, Rowan followed me inside.

"Are you going to tell me what the hell happened back there?" he said without preamble.

I slipped out of my heels and rubbed my feet. Not caring that Rowan was watching, I began stripping out of my dress, too. I just wanted to put on my pajamas and go to sleep.

"Anna—"

"Look, Rowan. I'm exhausted. Can we talk about this another time?" I slipped an oversized T-shirt over my head.

"No, we can't." Rowan's expression was grim. "Tell me what happened. Now."

I sighed. Being in my bedroom only reminded me of the last time we'd been here, and my cheeks heated. I didn't need that kind of distraction right now.

We went to the living room. I turned on a lamp and collapsed onto my favorite chair. Where did I even start?

I slowly recounted my conversation with Melanie. I avoided Rowan's gaze the entire time, because at the end of the day, I was a coward. When I got to the part about admitting I had feelings for him, though, I hesitated.

But I was tired of saying one thing and doing another. I didn't care if Rowan rejected me right here and now. At least I would know the truth.

"I told Melanie that I've fallen in love with you," I said softly.

Rowan was standing by my fireplace. I saw his fingers grip the mantel. But he didn't say anything. He was just staring into space.

"Melanie is convinced that you're going to treat me like you treated her. Although at this point, I don't know if she's genuinely concerned or if she's jealous. Maybe it's a little bit of both."

Rowan's nostrils widened. "And how, exactly, did I treat Melanie?"

"Seriously? Are we really playing a game of telephone here?"

Rowan leaned over me, his arms bracketing the chair and keeping me pinned there.

"What. Did. She. Say."

I gulped. "Um, that she wanted a commitment and that you froze her out. The end."

I couldn't tell what he was thinking. His eyes were dark,

his expression grim. It almost felt like I was looking at a man I didn't know. What had happened to the Rowan of earlier this evening, who'd whispered I was gorgeous as he brought me to orgasm?

"Then she neglected to tell you that when I wanted to leave my job and start my farm, she balked. She didn't want to live in the middle of nowhere. She thought I should stay in a job I hated, because it would be better for us." Rowan shook his head. "Really, it just meant more money for *her*."

"Look, I'm not interested in hearing the nitty-gritty details of your relationship with my best friend."

Rowan stood up. He ran his fingers through his hair. He'd already loosened his tie; his jacket was discarded somewhere inside his truck. He looked rumpled and delicious. He also looked like he wanted to be anywhere else but here.

"Whatever happened between you and Melanie," I said tonelessly, "it doesn't matter. Not really. But I lied to my best friend. And I hate myself for it."

I swallowed hard. "Yet I can't hate myself, because it brought me to you. I fell in love with you, Rowan. Because that part of the story? You didn't seem interested in that part."

"Are you fucking serious right now?" Rowan loomed over me now. "You think that 'part' doesn't matter to me? That I wouldn't care that you're in love with me?"

"Honestly, I don't know what's up or down right now. You look like you'd like to shoot your brains out."

"You have to understand. . ." He returned to the fireplace, resting his forearm on the mantel now. "Melanie wanted everything. She wanted the white picket fence, the wedding, the kids, the happily ever after. She expected *every-*

thing. And I couldn't do it. It felt like a death sentence when she told me she loved me."

I sighed. "Geez, dude, don't get carried away with your feelings—"

"But with you—" His eyes were a little wild now. "It's not a death sentence, hearing those words. It makes me want to give you everything."

My heart squeezed. I got up, needing to touch him. But his face seemed to tell me that I should stay away.

"So, what's the problem?" I whispered.

"I'm just going to disappoint you." He grimaced. "You'll want more and more and I'll try to give it to you, until one day you decide it isn't enough. It happened with Melanie. It's happened with my other exes. I survived all that. It was what it was. But the thought of that happening with you. . ."

Tears sprang to my eyes. "Why would it? I'm not your exes. And you're not the same man you were a year ago, even."

Rowan grabbed my hands and squeezed them. "I'm not going to let this go up in flames. It's better if we just end it now. Say goodbye, part as friends. And not expect anything else from each other."

Even though his touch was warm, I could barely feel it. Ice traveled down my spine. "You don't mean that."

He looked so sad now. "I'm sorry. I wish I could be that man for you."

Then he kissed my forehead, like he was consoling a child. I slapped his hands away.

"Then leave! If you're too scared to even try, that's on you. I'm not going to beg you to love me, to put some effort into this relationship. Whatever it is. But when you wake up, old and gray, and are all alone in this world, you'll know why. It'll have been your own fault."

Something dark crossed his face. "Goodbye, Anna Dyer. I wish you the best in life."

Then he left without another word.

CHAPTER TWENTY-ONE

ROWAN

When I showed up on my parents' doorstep a week later, I wasn't sure who was more shocked. Me, or them.

My mom gaped at me like she'd seen a ghost. "Rowan? Oh my word, Harold! Rowan is here!"

My mom was yelling so loudly that she was going to alert the entire neighborhood that I'd arrived. My parents still lived in my childhood home. Despite it being so familiar to me, there was always something about it that made it seem like it wasn't the same place I'd grown up in.

Maybe it was because my dad, always in need of a project since he'd retired, had gone a little crazy landscaping the yard. He'd dug up all the grass and had since replaced it with mostly ornamental rocks and succulents. He'd been one of the first in the neighborhood to do so. I couldn't help but notice that more of his neighbors had since gone "no-lawn" as well.

"Did something happen?" My mom fluttered around me like a worried moth.

In her late sixties, Sally Caldwell still looked great for her age. My mom still dyed her hair and was religious in her skincare regime. As a kid, she'd slather us with so much sunscreen that I'd look like a ghost at the swimming pool. But I had to admit, her sunscreen adherence had paid off. She looked like she could be in her forties.

"Nothing happened." I tried to sound upbeat.

Mom wasn't fooled. "Harold! Get in here! I don't know where your father is. He's probably listening to some gardening podcast. You know he figured out how to use his phone, and he's obsessed? But the man still won't use his debit card. I don't get it."

My dad finally came into the living room and gave me a once-over. Although I was hardly a kid anymore, I had to restrain myself from squirming under that gaze.

Dad could spot my weaknesses from a mile away.

You got a B- on your paper? You're smarter than that.

You didn't place at the track-and-field meet? You should've gotten up early to run like I told you to.

You're going into tech? And what happens when that bubble pops?

Of course, my dad hadn't counted on social media and smartphones taking over like they had. He'd assumed tech meant just another dotcom burst like in the early 2000s. But he never admitted when he'd been wrong. He simply didn't bring up the subject again.

"What's wrong with you?" Dad asked blandly.

"Why are you guys assuming something's wrong? I just wanted to see you guys. It's been a while," I said.

Mom shot Dad a glance that read, *Something's wrong.*

"You drove four hours to see your parents on a Thursday?" said Dad.

"Oh, did you miss us?" Mom hugged me tightly. "I was about to go down to Santa Clarita to see you. It's been too long. When is the last time you were here? Thanksgiving? That's too long." Her steely gaze pinned me to the spot as she added, "We're not getting any younger, you know. Next time you come we might not be here."

"Why, because you've moved?" I replied lightly.

Mom just shook her head. "Honey, you know we're getting older—"

"Sally, he's being deliberately obtuse." Dad narrowed his eyes at me. "You look like shit, you know. If anyone's going to croak soon, it'll probably be our son."

Mom gave Dad a look that told him he'd pay for that remark later. She then shooed him off, which he allowed with only some grumbling.

"I'm so glad you're here. Don't listen to your father. He's happy, too. He's just not good at showing it." Mom made me sit on the loveseat with her. "But I have to agree with your dad a little: you look tired. How are your oranges? Did you bring us some? I used up the last batch you gave us."

I suddenly felt like a complete idiot. When I'd gotten in my truck after making sure the farm would be attended to, I'd driven to Weston without even considering why.

I just had to get the hell out of dodge. Being at home only reminded me of Anna. Working on the farm also reminded me of her. Sometimes while working, I'd hear a voice, only to realize that I was alone.

So I'd come home to Mommy and Daddy because apparently my life was just that much of a fucking mess right now.

"Do you think Dad would be happy if I moved back here?" I asked.

Mom's eyes widened. "Rowan," she breathed. "Are you serious?"

"I'm considering it."

"Oh, sweetheart. He'd be thrilled. So would I. You could stay with us until you got your own place. I turned your bedroom into a home gym, you know, but you could stay in the guest room—"

"I'd get my own place," I said, shuddering inwardly at living with my parents for any length of time.

It wasn't that I didn't love my parents. I did. But while Dad tended to be cold and judgmental, Mom tended to overcompensate and be overbearing. She tended to smother me whenever I came home.

Which begged the question. . . Why had I come here when I didn't even really want to be here?

Because I'm a coward. Because I'm avoiding the inevitable. Because the thought of letting Anna go is tearing me up inside.

"I can set you up with Debra's daughter, Leah. I told you about her. She just got divorced. You'd be perfect together. She even has a house not even a mile from here."

Mom kept chattering away, not needing much of my input. I eventually let her know that nothing was going to happen for another year since I'd already committed to hosting a wedding at my farm.

Mom's shoulders fell. "Oh. A whole year? Well, I guess it'll go by quickly enough. . ."

"And I haven't made an official decision yet."

"Then I'll just have to do everything I can to convince you to move back home!"

AFTER WAKING up to the sound of Mom vacuuming the house at six a.m., I considered just getting into my truck and driving anywhere else. Maybe I'd go up to the Bay Area. I hadn't been there in years. Or I could keep going up to Oregon, Washington State. . . How easy was it to immigrate to Canada, anyway?

"Rowan, sweetheart, where's your dirty laundry?" Mom burst into my room without so much as a knock. "Oh, there it is. I'm doing a load of underwear. You and your father both have the smelliest boxers, I wonder if it's genetic—?"

I yanked the comforter over my head. How had I regressed to being thirteen again? *And why the fuck am I still here?*

While Mom was out shopping with a friend, I found myself alone in the house with Dad. It was too hot for gardening, so Dad was stuck inside. He puttered about the kitchen, making himself his usual bologna sandwich for lunch, while I sat and watched nothing on TV.

"What are you doing, son?" Dad asked me.

I muted the TV. "I'm visiting my parents."

"No, you're not. You're moping." Dad took a huge bite of his sandwich, then grimaced. "This light mayo is the worst. But your mother insists on buying it."

"You could always go to the grocery store yourself."

"I do. She'll just give away my mayo the first chance she gets." Dad looked me up and down. "What happened? Either tell me or go make yourself useful."

I leaned my head back over the couch and sighed. "I

fucked up. There, I said it. But you already knew that, didn't you?"

"I figured that. How about you tell me the details so I can make my own judgment?"

I scowled. Dad still could make me feel three inches tall. Was that just something parents gained the second their child came into this world?

I gave Dad the abridged version of what had happened with Anna. To my dad's credit, he didn't interrupt me once. He just listened and ate his sandwich in total silence.

"So I ended things," I said finally, shrugging. "And now I don't know what the fuck I'm doing."

Dad wiped his hands on a paper towel. "Did I ever tell you that your mother broke up with me before we got engaged?"

I stared in surprise.

"We don't really talk about it. She feels guilty about it." Dad shrugged. "But I don't blame her for it. I was an asshole. I acted like the sun shone out of my ass. So she set me straight and told me to go to hell." He chuckled, shaking his head. "When she told me she was leaving me, you could've knocked me over with a feather. I was completely blindsided."

As far as I knew, my parents had always been happy together. Sure, they were an odd match. I'd never understood why my mom put up with a man like my dad. He wasn't exactly romantic. Sometimes I wasn't even sure he liked his wife.

"So what did you do?" I asked.

Dad smiled wryly. "What do you think? I bitched and moaned for a bit until my brother knocked some sense into me. He asked me, 'Do you really want this to be the end?' At that point, I thought it was the end. But my pride was the one taking the reins right then. Realizing things could actually be over was unbearable.

"At any rate, I got your mom the biggest diamond I could afford—which wasn't much, if I'm being honest—and then went and begged her for forgiveness. Promised her everything and then some. And bless her soul, she said she'd take me back."

"I can't really see you going to anyone and begging," I admitted.

"She wasn't just anyone. She was the woman who was going to be my wife. I'd do anything for her. If this Anna girl is that woman, then you should go beg her for forgiveness. Do whatever it takes. Damn your pride. Pride doesn't keep you warm at night. Pride doesn't make sure you have dinner on the table or someone who gives a damn when you die."

I just dropped my head into my hands. "I don't think Anna will forgive me," I said. "She's not as nice as Mom is."

"Then you just have to try harder."

To my surprise, I felt Dad's hand on my shoulder. "Look, I'm not affectionate like your mom. Never have been. If I've been too harsh with you, well, it's only because I knew you could do better. And right now, you can do better than this. Don't disappoint me."

"Geez, Dad, don't lay on the guilt or anything."

"Whatever gets your ass out of my house. You're eating all the food. Besides, having you around interrupts private time with your mother."

I groaned. "Please stop. I'll go. Even if it's just to get you to stop talking about you and Mom."

Dad's face was serious now. "So? Do you love this girl?"

That question was like an arrow straight to the gut. I hadn't wanted to admit that I loved her. Admitting it meant that I'd have to do something about it.

Then again, hadn't I already sorta done something about it by sending Anna those drunken texts? Jesus, I'd fucked this whole thing from the start, hadn't I?

"Yeah," I admitted. "I love her."

"Well, there's your answer. You love her, she loves you. Go get her and don't let her go again." Dad leaned back in his chair, looking smug. "Also, just a tip: your wife is always right. Even if she's wrong. Just smile and nod. It'll get you through just about anything."

"She's not my wife." *Not yet, at least.*

I WENT HOME the next day. I didn't know what I was going to do to get Anna back. Sure, I could grovel and make promises and buy her hundreds of roses and buy the biggest diamond I could find. But would that be enough?

Anna wasn't the type of woman to be swayed by things like that. I'd have to prove it to her.

After I'd parked my truck and headed inside, I was startled when I heard a knock on my front door. My heart pounded. Was it Anna? But how would she know that I'd returned?

I opened the door, excitement making my blood thrum. But it wasn't a woman's face I saw: it was a man's.

Alejo was standing outside my door, looking sheepish. "Hey, man. You got a minute?"

"What are you doing here?"

"Pedro, he told me that you would be back today. So I came out and waited for you."

I frowned. "Are you stalking me?"

"You weren't answering my texts!"

I rolled my eyes. "Well, since you came all the way out here. . ."

Alejo followed me inside like a scolded puppy. He looked better than the last time I'd seen him, at least. I really didn't have the emotional juice to deal with Alejo crying over his fiancée a second time.

"When I heard you'd gone to your parents, I was surprised," said Alejo after I'd handed him a glass of water. "Are they okay?"

"What? Yeah, they're fine. I just needed some time away." I looked him up and down. "Did you make up with Emily?"

"Yeah. We're good now."

I couldn't help but feel a prick of jealousy at how happy Alejo looked now. Lucky bastard.

"Okay, so, why did you need to see me?" I asked.

Alejo blinked. "Did you not read my text?"

I shook my head. "I just got home and I was driving."

"You must be the only person on earth who doesn't text and drive. Anyway, Emily just got an email from Anna. She told us that she was not going to be planning our wedding anymore. She's found someone else for us."

The breath froze in my lungs. "What?"

"Yeah, it came out of the blue." Alejo rubbed the back

of his neck. "Emily feels terrible. She blew up at Anna recently—it was right after we'd fought—and she thinks this is why Anna quit. Anna said that wasn't the case, but it's hard to know what's true."

Alejo's gaze speared me. "I guess Anna didn't tell you, either?"

I felt cold all over. "No," I replied roughly.

"Emily was frustrated with Anna, I'll admit. She wasn't responding to emails like Emily needed, but we've been happy with her services overall."

"Anna? Not responding?" I had a hard time believing that.

"She'd just seemed really distracted lately. Or so Emily says. It was weird."

"Fuck." I got up and started pacing. "This is all my fault."

Alejo didn't look surprised. "Yeah, that's why I'm here. You're probably the only one who can convince Anna to come back."

My gut tightened. *Anna, what have you done?*

I replied, "I'm not so sure she'll listen to me. But that doesn't mean I can't make this right."

CHAPTER TWENTY-TWO

ANNA

Emily and Alejo looked at me like I'd told them I'd run over their dog.

"I promise you, Tricia will take amazing care of you. That being said, I'm also happy to provide you a list of recommended planners if you'd prefer—"

Emily leaned forward, nearly toppling her coffee over. "We told you, we don't want a new planner. What can we do to get you to stay?"

I stared at this couple, feeling like the lowliest worm alive. Yet I also knew I was making the right decision.

I couldn't keep working with Rowan Caldwell. At this point, being around him was a conflict of interest. I nearly lost Emily and Alejo as clients because I'd been so focused on my relationship with Rowan instead of on my business.

So what if I'd fallen in love? And so what if my heart was in pieces from being broken?

That didn't mean my livelihood had to fall to pieces, too.

I folded my hands in my lap. "There isn't anything you

can do or say to change my mind," I said slowly. "But I want to reassure you both that this has absolutely nothing to do with either of you. I've enjoyed working with you both greatly. I know your wedding will be amazing."

I swallowed against the lump in my throat. "I feel that right now, I can't be what you need me to be. That isn't fair to you. I refuse to be the reason your wedding isn't as magical as you deserve it to be. Because of those reasons, like I'd outlined in my email, I believe it's best if I step aside. I'll also refund you your deposit and a percentage of what you've already paid."

Alejo and Emily just looked at each other. I could feel the questions they wanted to ask me.

"If you're no longer our wedding planner," said Alejo slowly, "does that mean we can treat you like a friend?"

I blinked. "I guess so."

"Because we both know this has to do with Rowan."

When I flinched, Emily added quickly, "We understand. I mean, love is complicated. And Rowan is complicated. At least according to Alejo. I don't know him as well."

"I don't know if you want to hear this, but I just saw Rowan recently," said Alejo. He grimaced. "He looked like shit. He'd gone up and visited his parents for the past week in Weston. He's never liked going back to his hometown. So the fact that he'd impulsively leave his work behind to go to his parents. . ."

"I appreciate what you're trying to do, but Rowan and I are over." I smiled grimly. "He made that very clear. I'm not going to keep hoping he's going to have some revelation and come back to beg for my forgiveness." *Or to come back to tell me he loves me. . .*

"I can't speak to what Rowan will do, but he cares." Alejo's expression was serious. "I've never seen him this torn up about anyone."

After I said goodbye to Alejo and Emily, I sat at the same table, staring at my cold coffee.

Although I appreciated what Alejo said, at the same time, I hated him for it. It'd given me hope. Was Rowan really suffering without me?

I wanted to believe it. But wasn't it dangerous to hope when he'd already told me this relationship was over?

It didn't matter that I loved him. If he didn't want me enough to fight for us, I wasn't going to do the heavy lifting for him.

~

I STRUGGLED to get work done that afternoon. By dinnertime, I ordered Thai and collapsed in front of the TV to watch something trashy.

But as a stupid dating show came on, it reminded me of Melanie. For a brief time when we'd been roommates, we'd loved watching these types of shows together. We'd make it an entire occasion, with takeout, wine, and wearing our comfiest PJs.

I reminded myself that I was still mad at Melanie. We hadn't spoken since our blowup fight at Mia and Jackson's wedding. I hadn't even asked her why she'd been there.

But in that moment, with neither my best friend nor the man who'd become just as good of a friend, I felt unbearably lonely.

Sometimes I wasn't sure pride was worth being alone like this.

I scowled. *Don't be pathetic. Begging people to love you never works.*

As the dating show moved into love confessions, I had to change the channel to a horror movie. I didn't even like horror movies. But I needed something so unromantic that it'd take my mind off of my disastrous love life.

Murder All the Time Part 5 was hardly Oscar-worthy. My heart was pounding as I watched the idiot heroine peer around the corner to see if the murderous garbageman was still there. I was so engrossed that I nearly missed the knock on my door.

"Anna!" a voice called right at the same time the heroine screamed. And then I screamed, because what the actual fuck?

I nearly upended the entire bowl of popcorn I'd popped earlier. I was breathing hard, scrambling for the remote, when the voice called my name a second time.

I turned off the movie and stalked to my door. "What. The. Hell," I gritted out as I swung the door open.

Melanie stood there, looking abashed, even shy. She went so far as to avoid eye contact with me. I half-expected her to start twirling a strand of her hair around her finger.

"Can I come in?" she said, her eyes wide.

I considered tossing her out into the street. I looked her up and down. "Are you injured? Are you dying of cancer? If not, go away."

When I moved to shut the door, Melanie stopped me. "Please, Anna. I've missed you. Can't we talk at least?"

Right then, my elderly neighbor opened her door. She glared daggers at me and Melanie. "It's late," she intoned.

"Sorry, Doris." I then hissed at Melanie, "Get inside, you stalker."

Melanie at least didn't pilfer food from me this time. She even sat in my most uncomfortable chair and didn't so much as slouch. Her back was stick straight, like she was in etiquette class. She looked like she'd rather be anywhere else.

I, for one, lounged on my couch and waited for her to say something.

"You don't have to look so pleased with yourself," she sniped.

I smiled blandly. "Did you drive all the way here just to say that?"

Melanie huffed. I had to admit, she looked terrible: her hair wasn't perfectly brushed, she wasn't wearing makeup, and her clothes were rumpled. Had she been forced to go camping with a new, outdoorsy boy toy? I hoped she had. I hoped she'd had to sleep on the ground and that she couldn't sleep because bugs were crawling all over her.

"Stop looking at me like that!" Melanie yelled.

"How am I looking at you?"

"Like you've won. You haven't, by the way. I'm still mad at you."

At that, I sat up. "Well, spoiler alert, I'm still mad at you. I guess we're even. Now that we've confirmed that small detail—"

"Oh, stop acting like you're the victim here. We both fucked up. You lied to me. Multiple times. Did you really think I was so stupid that I wouldn't figure things out?"

"I lied because you made me lie." Now I just sounded childish.

Melanie gaped at me. "Seriously?"

"I mean, you backed me into a corner. I felt like I had to lie. I was working with Rowan, and then things were progressing, and it was like this unstoppable force."

Melanie just crossed her arms and glared at me.

I sighed. "If it makes you feel better, you were right. I think that's the worst part of all this. You were right about Rowan: he dumped my dumb ass the second I admitted my feelings. I said I love you, he said, 'Bye, bitch.'"

Even as I tried to sound chipper, my voice broke as the tears started. And then I was crying, because God knows I hadn't cried enough in the last seven days.

Melanie came to sit next to me. "I'm sorry. You didn't deserve that."

"Are you sure? I think it might've been karma biting me in the ass. I threw over my best friend for a guy. Not a great look."

"Maybe not, but I really didn't want to be right." When I gaped at her, she shook her head. "I'm serious! And maybe I overreacted because I knew, deep inside, that Rowan has never looked at me like he looks at you."

"Well, he's not interested in looking at me ever again. Don't worry about that."

Now Melanie was crying. "I'm so sorry. For everything. I should never have said what I said. I should never have made you promise. I was being selfish. But I think I was afraid I'd lose you. That Rowan would realize what an amazing woman you are, and then I wouldn't have a place in your life anymore."

Oh, geez. "That's the stupidest thing I've ever heard," I said, wiping my face.

"Well, I wasn't totally wrong, was I? You were going to choose Rowan over me in the long run."

"It's not about choosing one or the other. This isn't high school. We can still be friends even if I end up dating your ex-boyfriend from years ago."

"God, this all sounds like a soap opera."

I stifled a laugh. "Apparently, none of us can do things calmly and rationally."

Melanie was silent for a long moment. "What did Rowan say, exactly? When you told him you loved him?"

I didn't really want to recount this, but I swallowed the anxiety in my gut and told Melanie what had happened. Except for the bit where Rowan had told me Melanie had expected more from him than he could give. What was the point of telling her something that would just cause more hurt?

"You know, thinking about me and Rowan," Melanie began, "made me realize that we were never really compatible. He's too cold, too standoffish. I need more from a guy than that. I tried to make him into the guy I wanted. But it didn't work. It just made him want to leave."

I raised my eyebrows. Those statements were surprisingly emotionally mature for Melanie. My best friend, bless her, wasn't exactly known for deep introspection.

Melanie's gaze collided with mine. "But you two—you're perfect for one another. I can see that now. And I bet you a million dollars that Rowan is just avoiding you because he's scared shitless. If he didn't care so much, why would he be scared?"

"You're making a lot of assumptions," I said, trying to stifle the hope rising inside of me.

Melanie twiddled her thumbs. "If I'm being honest, our breakup wasn't because I loved him too much. I wanted a certain kind of life. He didn't. But I told myself it was because of the love thing. Nobody wants to admit they've been shallow.

"I can see on your face that you agree. So don't look so smug," she added with a huff.

"Once again, I'm not trying to look smug!"

"I think you should go after him. Then again, he's the one who needs to grovel." Melanie tapped her chin. "How can you get him to change his mind? Maybe just keep harassing him until he gives in?"

"I think that sounds like a recipe for a restraining order." I sighed. "No, I'll just have to wait. The ball is in his court."

Melanie leaned over and gave me a side hug. "He'll come around. I'm sure right now, he's just wallowing in complete misery. He's probably sobbing into a bucket of grapefruits—"

"Oranges."

"—fine, oranges. He's probably using the rinds to wipe his tears. Then he furiously masturbates while sobbing your name. 'Anna, Anna, I looooove you, oh, I'm coooooming—'"

I pushed Melanie aside. "Jesus lord above, woman, can you not?" Even as I said the words, I couldn't stop laughing.

Melanie just winked at me. "You know I'm right. We'll both just pray he's so miserable that he crawls back to you on his hands and knees."

CHAPTER TWENTY-THREE

ANNA

Weeks passed. I waited for Rowan's calls, texts, or even him dropping by my house. But there was nothing but radio silence. By the end of summer, I told myself that things were over between us.

He knew where I lived. If he'd wanted to contact me, he could have done so already.

I nursed my broken heart by eating a lot of tacos, crying in the bathtub, and writing out revenge fantasies about Rowan. Sometimes both. It depended on if I missed him or if I hated him more in that moment.

Fortunately, I had enough work to keep me occupied. One weekend, it was planning and attending a bachelorette party. The next, a wedding shower for nearly one hundred guests that I was fairly certain the bride barely even knew. Then one wedding, and then another.

The weekend before Labor Day, I spent my time sorting through favors for a bachelorette party that night. Which meant that I was making sure I had enough penis hats, penis straws, and matching shirts for all the attending guests.

We were going to a bar, having rented a private room, before taking the limo to the Sunset Strip for a Magic-Mike-esque show. I had a feeling that I'd have to be making sure a few guests kept their hands to themselves.

My doorbell rang. Getting up, I was surprised to see Alejo on my doorstep. How did he even know where I lived?

"Sorry, I know this is sudden," he said, "but I needed to talk to you."

"If this is about your wedding—"

"It is, kind of. But it's not about you becoming our planner again."

We went to the living room, where the various penis paraphernalia was strewn everywhere. Alejo, bless him, didn't seem too fazed by it.

He picked up one of the penis hats and said, "Should I even ask?"

"Bachelorette party."

He put the hat on, making me laugh. "How do I look?"

"Like you have a dick on your head." I grabbed the hat back, rolling my eyes. "Now, tell me why you're interrupting my very important work."

"Emily keeps telling me she's going to have a low-key bachelorette party. No strippers or anything. I think it's mostly because she doesn't want me to have strippers at my bachelor party."

"A no-stripper policy is generally a good idea, in my experience." I watched Alejo fiddle with one of the penis straws. "But I doubt you came here to discuss the merits of strippers versus no strippers at bachelor parties."

Alejo looked sheepish. "No, not really."

"I'd also like to ask how you knew where I live, but. . ."

"That was on Emily. She's the one with the sleuthing skills. But I thought this couldn't be discussed over the phone."

I raised an eyebrow.

"I found out that Rowan is selling the farm," Alejo said in a rush.

"What?" I stared at Alejo, waiting for the punchline of the joke. "You must've misheard. But what does this mean for your wedding? Do you have to find a new venue?"

"No, fortunately. Rowan assured us that the new owner is on board with turning it into a wedding venue." Alejo's gaze speared me. "But it's weird, isn't it? That you quit doing our wedding, and now Rowan is basically doing the same thing."

I felt my cheeks turn red. "I haven't spoken to Rowan in weeks."

"Well, I called him immediately when we got the email about the place changing hands. Then he asked if he could have his old job back at the tech firm where I work."

"But he left that job for a reason. Right?"

Alejo shrugged. "He never liked it. The farm was always his big dream. And he'd always said that although it was difficult, the business was doing well. Maybe it really wasn't. Or maybe something else changed. I don't know."

I didn't know how to respond to this news. *Rowan, what the hell are you doing?* It just didn't make any sense. He'd poured his heart and soul into that damn farm, and now he was selling it like it was no big deal?

"I also asked him point-blank if this had anything to do with you pulling out of our wedding," said Alejo quietly.

My chest tightened.

"All he said was that he wasn't going to stand between you and your business. Not anymore."

I couldn't take a full breath. I didn't understand what was happening. *It couldn't be. . .?*

After Alejo finally left, I sat in the middle of my living room, penis items surrounding me like a vulgar pentagram, and wondered what all of this meant.

Worse, I felt almost betrayed that he'd decided to sell without telling me. Which was stupid, because it wasn't like we were on speaking terms at the moment. It wasn't like he needed my permission to sell the place.

And then the traitorous thought: Was this his way of showing how much I meant to him? To relinquish his business, his beloved farm, because he really did love me?

I started crying. I was torn between hope and the fear that I was wrong.

Or was I just looking for signs that weren't even there?

A WEEK LATER, I was standing at the altar with my latest bride and groom, trying not to cry as they vowed eternal love for each other. Their French bulldog, Barnaby, who'd acted as their ring bearer, had decided I was his best friend. He sat at my feet after he came down the aisle, farting up a storm throughout pretty much the entire ceremony.

Holding my bouquet to my nose so I could avoid Barnaby's nuclear farts, I saw someone from the corner of my eyes stifle a laugh. Turning slightly, my gaze landed on a face I thought I'd never see again.

Rowan. Rowan was here.

My heart immediately began pounding like a drum. I couldn't even hear what the officiant was saying now. I just stared at Rowan, wondering if I was hallucinating.

He was wearing a gray suit with a light green tie, his hair shorter than when I last saw him. He'd even grown a bit of a beard. I was annoyed to notice that he looked fucking amazing.

Why can't you have gotten gaunt and spindly? Or have gone bald in my absence? But no, he had the audacity to look like a total snack when he should still be crying and masturbating while moaning my name like Melanie had said.

I turned my head away. This, however, only gave me a nice big whiff of Barnaby gas. I had to restrain myself from gagging. *What the hell did they feed this dog?*

Fortunately the ceremony was over soon after. Barnaby, being lazy now, didn't feel inclined to move from my feet. I ended up picking him up and handing him to a groomsman, who wrinkled his nose immediately upon contact with the stinky canine.

I didn't look at Rowan at all as I spread out the bride's train. I didn't look at him as we all walked down the aisle. And I definitely didn't try to get a glance in when we came back around near the ceremony space for picture time.

I avoided him throughout cocktail hour. I stayed with the wedding party, probably laughing more loudly than necessary at Uncle Pete's jokes. When the bride needed help going to the bathroom, I immediately volunteered.

Was I being a big scaredy cat? Yes. One hundred

percent yes. I needed to find my nerve before I spoke with the man who'd haunted my dreams for months now.

The man who I'd missed. The man who made my heart pitter-patter like a rabbit every time he was near. The man I loved but who'd broken my heart into a thousand pieces, too.

When I returned from the bathroom, though, Rowan found me.

"Anna," was all he said.

His voice stopped me in my tracks. Before he could say anything else, though, I gave him a cheerful smile and said, "Sorry, busy, talk later!"

I hurried away and proceeded to spend the first half of the reception dodging Rowan. It wasn't an easy task: the man was determined, I'd give him that.

When we got up to get in line for the buffet, he tried to butt in line. But the bride's granny nearly reamed him with her purse for daring to cut in front, so he had to slink to the back while everyone glared at him.

During dinner, he attempted to go up to the table where the bride, groom, and bridal party were all seated. I dodged him, however, going to the DJ and telling him we should start speeches now.

But I underestimated Rowan Caldwell. He didn't return to his seat this round. After the best man and the bride's sister made their speeches, Rowan snagged a glass of champagne from the table next to him and clinked it with a fork.

The crowd quieted down. I watched Rowan smile, his gaze fastened solely on me now. The bride leaned close to say, "Do you know that guy?"

"Ladies and gentlemen," Rowan began, his voice

sending shivers down my spine, "I first wanted to congratulate the new bride and groom. May you have an amazing life together."

The crowd cheered. I blew out the breath I'd been holding, thinking Rowan was done.

But he didn't sit down. He just waited for the guests to quiet, then continued, "I wasn't planning on doing this, but there's a woman here who's been avoiding me the entire wedding. Anna Dyer, I need to talk to you."

I felt everyone's gazes on me. Without getting up, I yelled, "We can talk later!"

"No, we're going to talk now." Rowan made his way toward our table. "Because you're going to dodge me all night long, aren't you?"

I just turned bright red in response.

"You see, everybody, Anna Dyer doesn't want to talk to me. I can't blame her, though." His gaze bored straight through me. "I messed up. I was a complete, and utter ass —" He cleared his throat. "—*jerk.* Sorry, trying to keep this PG for the kids here."

Now Rowan was standing right in front of me. "What I said that night: I didn't mean it. If I could go back in time and change things, I would. I can't, though. So from here on out, I'm going to do everything in my power to show you how much I love you."

I struggled to breathe. The bride was squeezing my arm, but I barely felt it.

"You love me?" I asked, my voice croaky.

"Yeah, I do." His lips quirked. "And it took me way too fu—sorry, way too long to realize it. You burst into my life like a whirlwind and set it all on fire."

"Thanks, I guess?" Then I remembered: "What about your farm?"

His smile turned sad. "I'd sell it five hundred times over if it meant you could keep doing what you love. And I'd sell it again, and again, and again, just to show you how much I adore you."

A collective sigh filled the room. Despite our audience, it also felt like Rowan and I were the only two people in the room.

Finally, I went around the table to Rowan. I took the microphone from him and said, "I love you, too, you idiot."

The crowd erupted into cheers. They got even louder when Rowan did a legit mic drop, dipped me over his arm, and kissed me.

And that kiss? It absolutely was *not* PG-rated.

CHAPTER TWENTY-FOUR

ROWAN

"Anna—Anna, wait—" I laughed as Anna nearly ripped my shirt from top to bottom. "We have plenty of time."

She growled. "Rowan Caldwell, it's been three months since I've even heard from you. Let alone slept with you. Either you give me some dick, or—" She screwed up her face. "I'll die, I guess."

"I'll give you the dick. I'll give so much dick you'll be begging me to stop."

"Oh, really? I like the sound of that."

I didn't know how we'd made it to Anna's house unscathed. We'd been a bundle of erotic energy the entire drive. It hadn't helped that Anna had unzipped my pants and had palmed my cock while I'd driven us. Worse, she'd even started to give me a blowjob before I'd begged her to wait.

"You don't think we should talk first?" I said.

Anna scowled. "Fuck now, talk later. Since when did you want to sit around and talk about your feelings?"

"A lot's changed since I met you."

Anna snorted and stroked my cock at the same time. "Not that much has changed. Although, is your dick a little bit smaller now—?"

I was the one growling now. I pounced on her, rolling her under me. She just laughed, and the sound made me want to beat on my chest in victory.

She was here. She was under me. She loved me, still. I didn't deserve it, but I wasn't about to look a gift horse in the mouth, either.

"For that remark," I said, my voice rough, "you'll have to be punished."

"Oh dear, how terrible, what shall I do—"

I covered her mouth with a kiss. She was right: there was too much talking right now.

I pushed her dress up, groaning when I discovered that she was only wearing a thong. "Surprised you're even wearing underwear," I remarked. I pulled the string of her thong and let it snap back against her pelvis.

She squeaked. "I prefer to wear something, but it depends on the dress."

"Fascinating." I shoved her dress up to reveal her lower half. "Tell me all about your panty collection as I rip this pair off of you."

"Please don't. This thong cost me at least forty dollars."

I gaped at her. "It's a piece of string."

"Women's lingerie is expensive. My bras are double that for one single bra."

I shook my head. I took her thong off—very, very gently—and then tossed it toward her closet. When she protested,

I said, "I'll buy you another one. Ten more. A hundred more. Whatever you want."

"Oh, well, if I can get whatever I want, then I want you to eat my pussy." She smiled widely. "Would that be acceptable to you?"

"I'll do that for free," I growled.

I spread her legs wide, my heartbeat getting faster as I gazed down at her already wet pussy. Then I buried my face in her folds, lapping and sucking and kissing until she was writhing under me.

I wanted to make her come over and over again. I wanted her juices covering my mouth, my chin, dripping down my face, marking me as hers. I wanted the scent of her pussy to cover my fingers.

"Rowan," Anna gasped. She arched, nearly bucking me off of her. "I'm gonna come—"

I fastened my lips around her clit. In just two more strokes of my fingers inside her, she came. She squealed. Her shudders made the entire bed shake. Growling, desperate, I rubbed the underside of my cock against the bedsheets.

As I was about to bring her to orgasm again, she pushed me up. "I need you," she said, making me shudder now. She kissed me. "Please."

She didn't need to ask twice. We finished undressing, and then Anna crawled on top of me. I watched in agony as she rubbed her pussy lips along my cock. The heat, the moisture—it was enough to make me come right then and there.

When she finally notched the head of my cock inside

her pussy, she leaned down and kissed me. I wrapped my arms around her.

"I got on my birth control," she breathed in my ear.

Fuck, what was it with her and forgetting to wear a condom? "I can pull out."

"No, I don't want you to." Anna started bouncing gently, my cock sliding in and out of her. "Fill my pussy up, Rowan."

Well, fuck, once again, she didn't have to ask me twice. It did take all of my willpower not to explode right then and there, though. It didn't help that Anna sat up, and I got to watch her breasts bounce as she rode my cock.

I pinched her nipples at the same time I thrust inside her. I watched in satisfaction as her eyes rolled back inside her head.

"Fuck, fuck, fuuuuuck." Anna quickened her pace. Her face was red, her chest flushed as well. Her eyes were glassy. She rode me harder and harder, groaning louder with each thrust.

I couldn't hold on. My balls drew up, and then I was coming in endless spurts, filling her pussy just like she'd asked me to. Anna moaned my name, and then she came, too. As her pussy gripped my cock, my own release continued. She drained me dry.

When she collapsed on top of me, neither of us could find the energy to move. We were sticky with sweat, pussy juice, and cum. I pushed Anna's hair away from her forehead, kissing her.

"Geez," she said, wheezing. She wiggled her hips a little, experimenting. "I'm tempted to keep going."

I groaned. "Christ, woman, you're going to kill me. Let a man catch his breath."

She laughed. I held her close, and then I was peppering kisses across her face, making her laugh. We rolled together, kissing like idiots, smiling like lovestruck fools.

I never wanted to leave this bed. I wanted to keep Anna Dyer right here, in my arms, my cock deep inside her, for all eternity.

ANNA BEGAN PLAYING with my chest hair, both of us on our sides now after we'd cleaned up. "Did you really sell the farm?" she asked.

I sighed. "The papers have been submitted, if that's what you're asking."

"So there's no going back?"

"I mean, there's a possibility I could stop the sale, but it'd be expensive."

"I don't want you to sell it. I know how much you loved it."

I pressed a kiss to her shoulder. "Not as much as I love you."

"Be that as it may, I don't want to be the reason you sacrificed your entire business. That's just depressing."

I snorted. "I considered it more like a grand gesture."

"And it is. I'm extremely impressed. I always thought you loved oranges even more than you loved me."

We lapsed into companionable silence. Although my mind had already given up the farm, I couldn't help but wonder if Anna was right. Maybe I should attempt to stop the sale from being finalized. Did I really want to give it all up?

I'd already mourned losing the farm. The thought I could get it back was like a ray of light, of hope, that I knew I didn't really deserve.

"Besides, I really did want to turn your place into a wedding venue," Anna added with a sly smile.

"I should've known there was something in it for you."

"Oh, come on. It's gorgeous. People love getting married in the middle of nowhere. Plus, it smells like oranges. And you could charge out the ass. Do you know how much people are paying just to rent wedding venues these days?"

"I already know what Alejo and Emily are paying me."

"And that's at a discount." I could practically see dollar signs in Anna's eyes. "Think about when it's up and running. I think I just had another orgasm thinking about it."

I snorted. "Considering it's about to be sold, don't get too excited."

She sighed. But I knew she was still scheming in that brilliant, evil little mind of hers. Even as it terrified me, I had to admit, I also loved it about her.

This woman would always keep me on my toes, that was for sure.

Anna began fiddling with the edge of the bedsheet now, which made me nervous.

"Spit it out," I said finally, feeling my anxiety rising with every second that passed.

"Um, it's not a big deal. But I talked to Melanie. We made up. No, no, don't give me that look. I'm not here to rehash your relationship. No, thank you. But I'm also a little worried. . ."

"About?"

"It seems like when things get tough, you shut down. You walk away. You stuff your feelings in some box and bury them six feet under." Anna glanced at me under her lashes. "And you can't deny that's true, because that's what you did three months ago."

I wanted to do exactly that right then. I wanted to kiss Anna to make her shut her mouth. Instead, I clenched my jaw and just listened.

"I guess I just want to know that you'll work on that. I have things I need to work on, too. Don't get me wrong. But if something feels overwhelming, please don't disappear. At least, not for three months." Her eyes were shiny with tears now. "That hurt too much."

I brushed the hair from her forehead. "I can't promise I'll always do the right thing, but with you, I want to try. I want to do better. I don't want to leave you in the dust. If it makes you feel any better, I was miserable for three months. I missed you every single day. I was glued to my phone, waiting for you to text me. It was torture."

She smiled sadly. "Same. When I'd hear my phone go off, I'd keep hoping it was you. Speaking of which, I should really have a separate phone for business calls and messages. . ."

"I'd like to ask one last thing of you, though."

"Shoot."

I pulled her into my arms. "Never mention Melanie's name while we're in bed again. From here on out, it's just you and me."

Anna's smile made my own heart burst with ridiculous, overwhelming joy. "Deal."

EPILOGUE

ANNA

As I watched Alejo and Emily dance for their first song, the scent of oranges filling the warm, summer air, I wondered how I'd gotten so lucky.

"Alejo looks like he's about to faint," Rowan whispered in my ear. "Apparently Emily had to drag him to dance lessons and somehow his dancing skills only got worse after that."

"He's doing fine," I whispered back. If I noticed Emily wincing when he stepped on her feet, I wasn't about to point it out.

The day after Rowan and I had gotten back together, he'd gone a little crazy. He somehow managed to stop the final sale of the farm—at least with his original buyer. He'd then returned to my house with an envelope of documents without so much as a "hello, do you want to buy my farm?" before setting them down in front of me.

We'd negotiated for weeks. Rowan, despite being my boyfriend and one true love, apparently didn't think I deserved to be given an easy ride.

"Can't you just give me fifty percent?" I'd demanded as the negotiations had drawn out.

"And what fun would that be?" he'd replied, smiling evilly.

We'd eventually reached a deal that worked for both of us. It also split the farm into two separate businesses: one for the grove itself, the other for a wedding venue. Rowan would run the former, I would run the latter, but we'd have stakes in both.

The next year had become a whirlwind of weddings, venue preparations, licenses, inspections, and a whole lot of logistics. Did I sell my house and move in with Rowan? I'd been reluctant, only because I didn't want to live in the middle of nowhere. Rowan had eventually agreed to live in my place and spend a few nights a month at the farm.

And now we'd just watched Alejo and Emily vow to love each other for eternity. Even better, I'd hired another wedding planner that had taken over the reins of actually coordinating couples' weddings. So I could simply sit back and enjoy the show as a lowly bridesmaid.

When the first dance ended, we all applauded, Alejo looking immensely relieved.

"Do you ever think about our wedding?" asked Rowan as we waited to be served dinner.

I gaped at him. "Are you seriously asking me that right now? Please tell me you aren't proposing at someone else's wedding."

He looked surprised. "People do that?"

"Yeah, assholes do."

"Well, no, I wasn't going to propose right now. Or soon. Unless I should—" Now he looked like he would rather jump in the nearest river than complete that sentence.

I patted his arm. "Babe, we can have this discussion at another time." I smiled widely. "Besides, when we do get married, it's going to be the most amazing wedding this city has ever seen."

"Oh, God. I've created a monster."

"I know you don't like a dove release, but what about a moment where two hawks fly to us? Oh, and maybe releasing thousands of butterflies. That'd be amazing. What are your feelings about fish in vases? We could do those huge centerpieces and fill them with Betta fish—"

Rowan was looking greener by the minute. "Anna, please."

I just grinned. "I'm kidding. Well, except for the hawk bit. I saw it done at another wedding, and it was amaaaazing."

Rowan, being smart, changed the subject after that. We were too busy stuffing our faces, dancing, and drinking cocktails. It helped that the couple's friends and families knew how to throw a party. Even Alejo's abuelas got on the dance floor and danced until the wee hours of the night.

As Rowan and I danced a slow dance, he said quietly, "I've been thinking about our wedding, you know."

I raised an eyebrow. "Oh, really? Are we getting married?"

"That's a dumb question." He squeezed my ass. "Of course we're getting married. Maybe not any time soon. But eventually."

"Okay, so it's definitely happening. What were you thinking about?"

"Well, mostly at first I was thinking about you wearing a garter that I'd take off with my teeth—"

"Your confidence never ceases to amaze me."

His expression turned serious. "But then I thought about how you'd look walking down the aisle toward me. And then I realized that none of the other stuff mattered. Doves, hawks, butterflies, fish, whatever. None of it would compare to watching you come toward me and then us vowing to love each other forever."

I had to wipe away a stray tear. Damn the man. He knew how to make a girl feel special.

"I think about that, too," I admitted. "Mostly I wonder if you'll cry."

Rowan's face turned to stone. "I never cry. Don't get your hopes up."

"Oh ho ho, is that a challenge? Bet you I could get you to cry. If we get a string quartet play 'I Can't Help Falling in Love' and I'm looking gorgeous in a white dress as our eyes meet? You're telling me you wouldn't shed one single tear?"

"No. Not one."

"I don't believe you. I think you'll blubber like a baby."

Rowan looked annoyed now. "You're the one who's gonna cry."

"That's definitely true. But we're not talking about me. And I'm going to do everything in my power to get you to cry. You do realize we'll be writing our own vows, right?"

He groaned. "Christ, woman, you love to make me suffer, don't you?"

"Yeah, but only because I love you so much."

"I love you, too." Rowan squeezed my ass a second time. "Now, if you're done talking, how about we break out of this joint and go have a quickie in the barn? Because you're looking so sexy in that orange dress of yours right now."

I laughed at him, kissed him, and then let him lead me to a dark corner to do unspeakable things to me, because I just loved this ridiculous man that much.

ABOUT THE AUTHOR

A coffee addict and cat lover, USA Today bestselling author Iris Morland writes sparkling, swoon-worthy romances, including the Flower Shop Sisters and the Love Everlasting series.

If she's not reading or writing, she enjoys binging on Netflix shows and cooking something delicious.

She currently lives in Seattle with her partner, two cats, and an excessive number of houseplants.

Made in the USA
Monee, IL
10 October 2022